I0661536

Chester Bailey Fernald

The cat and the cherub, and other stories

Chester Bailey Fernald

The cat and the cherub, and other stories

ISBN/EAN: 9783337220464

Printed in Europe, USA, Canada, Australia, Japan

Cover: Foto ©Andreas Hilbeck / pixelio.de

More available books at **www.hansebooks.com**

THE CAT AND THE CHERUB

Grace Wetherell

THE
CAT AND THE CHERUB
AND OTHER STORIES

BY

CHESTER B. FERNALD

NEW YORK
THE CENTURY CO.
1896

Copyright, 1895, by
C. B. FERNALD

Copyright, 1895, 1896, by
THE CENTURY CO.

THE DE VINNE PRESS, NEW-YORK

CONTENTS

THE CAT AND THE CHERUB

THE CAT AND THE CHERUB

IVE were the years of the Infant Hoo Chee, and five were the inches of his cue. Then he had an adventure.

Every one in San Francisco who loves to look at a beautiful girl remembers Bayley Arenam. Once you mention her among the Hundreds straightway springs some novel anecdote of a cleverness of hers. She was a Californian, blessed with a glitter of talents and with a person to vex the gods. And she was the one.

Hoo King was the Infant's father — the ginseng merchant; and Hoo Bee, of the lily feet, was his mother. She who tended him was Hwah Kwee, the amah, a woman of flat feet and considerable kindness. They dwelt in Chinatown and prospered there; for Hoo King had interests, and was one of the secret Ho Wang Company, and was greeted with smirks at the Hong-Kong-American bank.

The Infant's world was three wide rooms on a topmost floor, — commodious, truly, — and a flower-pot balcony leaning over the main thoroughfare, whence one could drop beans on passers-by, and run away in an ecstasy of fear. Only at intervals did he see the streets; and then he was wedged between the amah and his father, both inwardly alert. For the fifth of

1

Hoo Chee's years was a troublous time and made history in the quarter; and one who would strike most bitterly at Hoo King, the suspected traitor to the Chee Kung Tong, would take, not the old man's life, but his son. The parents treasured their offspring because his existence insured the rightful worship at the graves they expected to fill; and so they made a baby of the boy, though he was of the age when some sons put on cue-strings and a man's estate; and they tried to discourage fascinations beyond the threshold. But every day the Infant saw the forbidden streets with deeper longings.

His only human friend was Yeo Tsing, the Presbyterian evangelist. Yeo had a pious, folded look, as of a holy volume; but he had a genial eye for a child. He taught the Infant many mission songs, which Hoo Chee caught from the convert's lips and held tenaciously, especially the air of that hymn which inquires pertinently of all little Chinese proselytes, first in a high and skeptical tenor,

> Are you washed — are you washed?

and then in a bass and warning tone,

> Are you washed — are you washed?

and so forth. This the Infant was fond of singing to himself, though there is doubt whether he could have expounded it theologically.

But best of all, Yeo served to tide over some of the child's depression with telling him stories — stories of small people who did great things. The one that

appealed to the Infant most was that of a little boy
who set out from home all alone, and after many,
many weary miles, and countless trials in which he
showed exceeding fortitude and virtue, arrived at a
glorious place called the House of Glittering Things,
where he lived happily ever afterward. It was not
very clear why the little boy had left home. Yeo could
never be quite satisfactory on that point, because he
had forgotten about it, and was too honest to invent.
But what conditions would lead a little child to go forth
from the roof of his birth and return no more, the Infant knew well in his heart, and kept there. He had
learned from these stories much to whet his cravings
for the world outside. It seemed that there were re-
gions where, as far as you could see, all the land was
like one great back yard, except that instead of musty
boards and grim, gray rubbish there were acres and
acres of waving green things, and millions of beautiful flowers that you might pluck without a whipping
— flowers as handsome as those on the balcony, and
free for all! And there were places where a hundred
roof-spouts could not make so big a puddle as was
spread as clear as crystal earrings in a circle of these
posies, where humorous little things with legs were
waiting to jump head first into the water just as you
almost touched them, and then to laugh at you from
the opposite bank; and where little fishes from behind a rock peeped up at you out of the corners of
their eyes.

When the Infant was by himself he would describe
all these things to little One-Two, his beloved cat and
confidant, the only creature with whom he divided his

sorrows. One-Two was barely out of kittenhood, yet
had a vague, inviting melancholy in his look. Most
of his body was covered with long white hairs that
spoke of Angora; but his tail was slim and bluish-
gray, and altogether Maltese; and when one remembers how he appeared suddenly from nowhere, and
came mewing, cold and lean and hungry, into the joyous arms of the Infant, it is not hard to imagine One-
Two as the projection in time of an international
romance. The Infant coddled the waif and stole food
for it, and named it One-Two because it had one tail
immediately prominent as an error in its composition,
and two eyes of imperial yellow. These were its salvation, for Hoo King had at first superstitiously commanded that the strange cat be dismissed; but Hoo
Chee had resisted even to struggles and tears, which
tenacity delighted his father, who at once asked a fortune-teller for a translation of the omen. If the cat's
eyes were blue, came the dictum, then boil its body in
oil, for the augury was bad; but if they were the
color of the viceregal jacket, then it was a cat of fortune better than good. So One-Two survived, and
slept curled in the Infant's arms, and perpetually followed him about in the daytime, and waxed in size
until he was heavy to carry. Once from his balcony Hoo Chee saw a little American girl — one of
delicacy rare in this quarter — going along the street
bearing a cat. It was not so pretty as One-Two,
thought the Infant; but it had a red ribbon around
its neck that gave it too much honor. He searched
his world for something like the red ribbon; but there
was nothing. At last he abstracted from his mother's

possessions some bright-green silken cords that looked
like cue-strings, and he made a little cue of the long
hairs of the cat's neck, and braided in the silk as an
extension of it. One-Two, whose mischosen tail was
already a source of questioning self-contemplation,
spent a bad half-day in a corner, foreboding over this
fresh phenomenon. To Hoo Chee the effect of the
trailing green was rhapsodical, and the event of happy
hours.

But ever his confinement from the glowing world
told on the Infant's years. The shouts of thousands
of Freedom's Aryan children penetrated to his small
body and infused in it some of the New World es-
sence. Now came the season of the Chinese New
Year, and he remained stalled with three impassive
spirits, while the air about was joyous with music
and laughter and song. He could not play by day
when from his rear window he caught a bare glimpse
of the Taoist priests, led by a string of pompous
boys,— some of them seemingly smaller than he,—
all making way to the joss-house, bearing gifts to the
gods, and making the quarter resound with squealing
pipes and clanging gongs. He could not sleep by
night when everywhere he heard invisible fire-crack-
ers rattling as if the gods had come down. While
the amah snored by his side he lay awake and
thought of the story of little Quong Sam and the
House of Glittering Things, and the lovely lady
that made him tea and gave him cakes whenever he
asked. He longed to go abroad and meet with like
adventures.

The sixth day of the holiday week had been set for

1*

what happened but once a year. It was a trip away
from the quarter,— first to the cemetery, and then to
the ocean beach,— to which the women looked forward with highest delight. Hoo Chee had learned
some time before that they were to take him along,
and this had sent him singing and dancing the rest
of the day. But it seemed that the time would never
come. When Hoo King came in one morning and
found the women bedecked in their best, he suddenly
changed his mind, and said that the child should re-
main at home, and that the amah must stay to take
care of him. For a father with a single offspring it
was too extravagant a risk to take a small child on a
railroad train among the foreign devils, whose curiosity and impertinence at the sight of the women
were themselves enough to bear. They had dressed
the Infant handsomely; he was sure that this was
the momentous day, and his blood ran gaily at the
prospect; but again they told him the time had not
yet come, and the father went off with Hoo Bee,
leaving the amah weeping behind. It was the cus-
tom of the amah to weep, and the child felt sure
they would have taken her if this was the wonderful event. He went to his favorite place on the
balcony, only somewhat hushed and downcast.

He was thinking, though he did not know it. Why
did they always keep him in, instead of letting him
loose, as he saw the happy little urchins in the street?
Could he not go about boldly enough, and preserve
himself as well from harm as they? When would
they braid silk strings in his curtailed pigtail, and
put his head in a cap with a red button, and his legs in

splendid sky-blue trousers wrapped at the bottoms?
Certainly he was already as strong as any man. He
could kick off all the bed-clothes, and get spanked
for it by the amah. He could hang by his ankles to
the edge of the sink, and appear to be standing on
his head. The amah would not dare such a feat.
And during all this festal period they had taken him
out only once — then briefly to the joss-house, before
the hairy wooden gentlemen who sat receiving offerings of fruits and sweets enough to make a covetous
infidel of any mortal. He was charged to repeat
certain words that he could not understand to the
wooden gentlemen, which he did with an accuracy
flattering to his father. But then they dragged him
unwilling home through the decorated streets, with
the thrauneen of a rice-cake as his part of the re-
joicings.

One-Two had cautiously picked his way over the
iron bars to a seat on a flower-pot, whence he licked
the hand of his small patron. But now the Infant
was staring down across the street like a statuette.
He had seen Miss Arenam. This was the third time
he had feasted his big brown eyes on her. Occasionally, after an absorbing morning with the clay, she
left the lunch-room at the art school, and strolled
through as much of Chinatown as included the principal windows, where new things are sometimes found
in porcelain and bronzes. He had noticed her first
when she paused one day in curiosity at the balconies
on his side of the street. He had stared in fascination, with his chin on the rail; and then from as far
as he could strain outward without falling he had

watched her moving away. Two months later she
appeared again. She did not look up this time, and
after a minute the Infant shouted, "Ha-o!" But his
small voice was inadequate, and she departed without
noticing. Now the lovely dark-haired lady had
shown herself once more. The Infant was absorbed
in thought, and his eyes were fixed constantly on the
door of the china-shop whence she would soon emerge.

After a while he could see her skirts moving about
in the store, and then—there she was!

"Ha-o!" cried the Infant, swinging his arms up
and down.

Then he stood mute and discontented, for she had
not looked up, but had walked away quite unaware
of him.

Was he always to stay thus pent? If he were free,
how quickly he would run and get her to smile! The
amah had left the room. He could hear her down-
stairs, communing in bitter tones with the neighbor
Ching Lo. From the threshold of the forbidden hall
he heard no noises — every one who could go out was
on the streets. On such a day as this, perhaps, the
brave little Quong Sam of old had ventured forth to
find the House of Glittering Things. The Infant
grasped the baluster with every sense alert, and took
one step down. No angry lightning came to strike
him. Then he took another step, and paused to listen
if there were bad devils coming to seize a naughty
boy. But the house was still, and he went on, planting
two feet safely on each step until he reached the landing. Ching Lo's door was ajar, but not so that they
could see him; and his soft shoes carried him noise-

lessly past. There, down another flight, was the street
—and then he could run and catch the lovely lady!
He made the descent to the front door with greater
confidence and equal circumspection. How delightful the free air! Now he would hurry and ask her
the way to the House of Glittering Things, for she
must know, if, indeed — why had he not thought before? — she were not herself the Lady of Cakes and
Tea! Oh, joy! Then he heard a familiar voice that
stopped him. It was One-Two, who had followed
him, and now stood questioning at the head of the
flight. He had almost forgotten One-Two; but could
he leave the faithful partner of his woes behind?
The Infant stood in serious quandary. That his
father would be interested in his son's disappearance
did not occur to the child. No such idea had been
instilled in him. But indeed the loss of One-Two,
the mascot, would not be undergone without long
search and deep displeasure. You could buy little
boys at a joss-house, but mascots came only unexpectedly in through the window. Yet should One-
Two stay on and fall again to the bad grace from
which he had so recently emerged, the Infant shuddered for what might happen. For the cat would be
thrown from a window into the soiled back street.
But still, with such a burden, how weary would the
many miles be on the way to the House of Glittering
Things! And he remembered how little Quong Sam
had not only cast away his shoes, but had even
shaved off his eyebrows to make himself lighter for
his feet to carry. Now came another complication —
he must ascend the stairs to get One-Two, who re-

fused to come down, as though mistrusting the ad-
venture — One-Two, who had been upon the world
and knew it; and if the amah heard but one suspicious sound, she would rush out and end his prospects
for days and days, and the lovely lady would be lost
to him.   But One-Two put his fore feet down one
step, and stood with his hind quarters elevated and
his tail waving, loyal to indissoluble ties, and Hoo
Chee saw it even while he pondered the problem.
And now, when the cat opened wide his mouth, and
without a noise plainly showed the first anxiety about
the plighted faith, it was too much: he loved One-
Two!

The Infant crawled stealthily on hands and chubby
knees up the stairs.   One-Two advanced carefully to
meet him, and was taken into the arms of the child,
who silently, in his clumsy baby fashion, made way
with his burden back to the door, and out to the
street.

Miss Arenam was standing at the summit of the
hill, looking over the dingy housetops down to the
bay, which shone in the sun like a strange enamel set
in mountains.   He recognized her figure and the color
of her dress.   He would hurry up the steep incline
and go with her.   He would find little Quong Sam,
and play with him in the Glittering House; for,
though it was a thousand years since Quong had
started forth, who that had come to the presence of the
Lady of Cakes and Tea would ever care to leave it?

He passed other children playing about uncared for.
They were dressed in common garb, but he was in his
best.   He wore little shoes with white felt soles, and

uppers embroidered in gold, to which came long, loose, drab-colored trousers. A skull-cap worked in spangles and prodigal hues came down to his ears, and through a neat hole in its crown projected his cuelet, curling away like coal-black smoke from a wigwam. His bulky tunic, which reached to his knees, was covered with a gingham bib tightly tied with tapes at the hips, so that he swelled out hugely above and below the waist. When he walked his arms seemed lost in his clothes, and his knees bobbed strangely up and down.

Ah, but the hill was steep! Now he understood how the youthful Quong had toiled and toiled and been discouraged; but Hoo Chee should not quail, though heavy One-Two must be changed so frequently from arm to arm. He came to a crossing where a traction cable rattled terrifically; and he ran as fast as his legs would go to escape the car that was coming three blocks away. They had said he did not know!

But the lovely lady had slowly walked away, and was lost immediately behind the brow of the hill. Was he going to miss her? No! He tried to run up the incline, and his little heart beat faster and faster. At last he reached the top, and saw the hem of her blue skirt swish around a corner. Now it was level going. He caught his breath, and trotted as fast as he could, unaware of the people who turned and smiled.

When Miss Arenam had gone a few steps down the other side of the hill, on the sharp descent from the nabob castles, and had started up the flights of stones that led to her father's house, she caught first sight of the Infant. He had paused, and now gazed at her

in a mixture of doubt and bashfulness. His tiny figure, silhouetted against the sky at the line of the hill-
top, was the most entrancing thing her eyes had met
that day. She smiled across the little distance, and
the Infant smiled in response. When she looked
again, from farther up, Hoo Chee was hurrying after
her; and in a moment he could stare mutely up at her
with his hand on the open gate.

"Hello, little gentleman!" said Miss Arenam;
"won't you come in — and bring your friend?"

The Infant could not speak her tongue, but her smile
was better than words. He tucked One-Two under
his arm, and labored solemnly up the steps with hand
and feet, until he halted to gaze in rapture at her from
nearer than he ever had dreamed. Miss Arenam,
shining down upon him, threw open the door; and
the two went in together, the silent Infant staring at
her in such intense admiration that she blushed.

By this time the pallid Hwah Kwee was rushing
about in breathless search of her lost charge. There
was no sight of him. She dared not say she had lost
him; for if no one knew he might wander safely back,
but if it were noised abroad some one would snatch
him up.

"What shall I do?" wailed the amah to Ching Lo.
"He has strayed into the vast maze of the city. Hoo
King will kill me!"

"Say that he was stolen — that they knocked you
senseless."

"But he will see no mark from the blow," said the
amah.

"Make one! It is better than a thousand from the old dragon."

Hwah snatched a broken dish, and struck its jagged edge against her forehead.

"Leave the wound alone!" cried Ching Lo. "Go and lie in a heap near your door, and think what you will tell the master. I will say I heard terrible sounds, and thought he was beating you."

"If I can only keep him long enough to get his darling little noddle, I shall be celebrated," said Miss Arenam, working rapidly over a moist clay ball. The Infant sat on a stool at her feet, holding a fold of her skirt, and eyeing her intently. One-Two was lapping a dish of cream, and meditating on the exceeding wisdom of this small boy. Frequently Hoo Chee and the girl exchanged smiles.

"But, Bayley," said her mother, "we must find whose child he is. Think of the mother who is weeping for him!"

"I've sent for Gee, mama," said the daughter. The clay was taking something the shape of the little noddle in question. Gee, summoned from the kitchen, threw up his hands.

"Whey you catch that baby? Who b'long, Miss Bayley? Oh, no! I doan' like go Chinatown say I know whey that baby was. People say I stolee that baby — make baily, baily bad for me. Whose boy are you?" asked Gee, in Chinese.

"Ha, ha, ha!" laughed Hoo Chee, throwing back his small head, and pulling at the lady's skirt. It was not plain what amused him.

"Now, Gee," said Miss Arenam, "I wish to ask him some questions."

The servant translated, "What is your name, small sir?" The Infant thought the query originated with Gee.

"Flower-pot," replied the Infant, with a giggle.

"And what is your father's name?"

"Water-pot," said Chee, with another giggle.

"And your mother's?"

"Rice-bowl!" shouted the Infant. Then he laughed loud and long, while his fat little body shook. Only the Chinaman preserved gravity.

"That baby baily small baby, but great much tell lies — allee samee 'Melican boy."

"I will send a note to the police station," said Mrs. Arenam, "and ask them to inquire in Chinatown."

"I hope they won't find out anything until I have finished this — as long as he is happy here. I don't think his parents will worry over him. What an *objet d'art* he will be for the people this evening!"

"Bayley, your heart is turning to clay with all this mud-work. Suppose you had a little son, and he should stray away! I dare say it will be some time before his father thinks of asking the police. Those Chinese are so stupid about some things. If that child is to stay here this evening he must be scrubbed. Gee, I want you to give this boy — if it is a boy — a bath."

"Oh, no! I no likee. S'pose he die? That baby not old enough to wassee."

"Send for Mrs. Brady, mama," said Bayley.

Miss Arenam went on with the modeling. The In-

fant was still for several moments, while the young
woman frowned, and stood off from the clay, and
measured his nose with her little stick, which opera-
tion he considered most delightful. It was plain that
he was involved in a mental process. At length he
lisped doubtfully :

"Pay-lee ?"

"Yes, dear," said Bayley; "that is my name."

"Pay-lee," said the Infant, confidently. He began
to move about the room, so that she had difficulty in
working from him.

"Come here, little man," she said; "I'll teach you
some English. Say this : 'Infinitesimal James'—say
it : '*Infinitesimal James!*'"

"' 'If-itty-teshi-mow Jays,' " repeated the Infant.
The two smiled ecstatically at each other.

"Now say : '*Had nine unpronounceable names.*'"

"' 'Haddee ny up-plo-now-shi-buh nays '—ha! ha!"
laughed Hoo Chee. It was a rhyme—like those he
had heard his father say to Yeo Tsing.

"Now : '*He wrote them all down.*—'"

"' 'He lote im aw dow',' " repeated the Infant. One-
Two looked on from near by. Hoo Chee stood with
his hands on Miss Arenam's knee, staring straight
into her eyes.

"' '*With a mortified frown,*—' "

"' 'Witty motti-fy flow,—' "

"' '*And threw the whole lot in the flames!*'"

"' 'A-flew-ty ho-lot-itty flays!' Hee!"

Very soon he could repeat the lines without prompt-
ing; and meanwhile Bayley was deftly shaping in
the soft ball two almond eyes, and a little flat nose,

and a mouth that opened in a smile, and was to show teeth as big as grains of rice. The Infant was enchanted by the rhyme, and kept on repeating: "If-itty-teshi-mow Jays" with happy countenance. Then Bayley taught him another verse:

There was a little boy, and he was n't very bright, and
  He could n't tell his left from his right hand;
So he chawed his dexter paw till the skin was red and raw,
  To remember that the right was the bite hand.

Then a stout, clear-skinned woman came to the door, and held a brief conversation with Miss Arenam, who suggested that Hoo Chee go along with the nice lady and enjoy a bath. Mrs. Brady held out her big hand to him. But the Infant grappled with all his might to Miss Arenam's skirt, and exclaimed his objections in a volume of Chinese baby-talk. He and One-Two willingly followed Miss Arenam into the tank-room, however, and she left him there with Mrs. Brady, closing the door rather quickly. There was a sound of running water, and Hoo Chee, between the blue mermaids on the tiles, and curiosity at what was to happen in this big, warm room with nothing in it but a square porcelain pond, seemed to have forgotten his anxiety, especially when the pond began to fill with water, and he searched it earnestly for little fishes that looked up from the corners of their eyes.

Miss Arenam stood in her apron, and hummed to herself, while she gave the roughly outlined bust little dabs with her forefinger. Suddenly there came

a frantic shriek from the tank-room, and, hurrying in
that direction, she heard a small voice shrilling in the
direst fear:

"Pay-lee!   Pay-ay-ay-lee!"

"What is the matter?" she asked, knocking at the
door.   "Have you scalded that child, Mrs. Brady?"

"Scalded um!" said Mrs. Brady, from the other
side.   "I've just hoisted um into the water, an' he
won't let go me neck.   *Take yer han's from me hair,
ye little imp!   Did ye never see water?*"

"Pay-lee!" shouted the Infant, who apparently
held the situation under control.   The top of the tank
was on a level with the floor, and Mrs. Brady had to
kneel to it.   But then a splash was heard, and the
anxious Bayley, at the door-knob, was frightened by
another mighty screech.

"Mrs. Brady," protested the girl, tapping the panel,
"I am sure that water is too hot; perhaps he is not
used to hot water."

"Or cold, either," puffed Mrs. Brady, turning the
faucet.   "*Put yer foot down!* (Maybe if ye stay there
an' talk he'll be peaceful.)   Take it out of yer mouth
—it ain't sody-water!   Oh, I wish I was yer mother
—no, I don't!   Now, here comes the shower!"

Bayley heard the pattering of many drops, and
through them, as from a lamb in a rain, many sounds
in Cantonese, with the wail of "Pay-ay-ay-ay-lee!"

"There, Mrs. Brady!   You must have let that water
'un too long; perhaps he's chilled."

"Hot it is," came the answer; "an' the responsibil-
ty be with you.   *Now!*   Maybe if you'd go away he'd
be quiet."

2

There came a mixture of scrubbing and yells that increased as Hoo Chee found that he was not hurt, and began to express his anger. He seemed in the tortures of purgatory.

"What in the world *are* you doing to that child to make him cry so?" said Bayley.

The bath-brush came with a thump to the floor, and there was an instant of silence.

"Did n't ye tell me to wash um?" said Mrs. Brady, as if the whole matter might have been a mistake.

"Of course I did!" said the girl, with much warmth.

"Well, I 'm *washin'* um!" said Mrs. Brady, with equal emphasis; and the scrubbing continued. "D' ye think I 'm tattooin' um? Now he 's done it! He 's put a fistful of soap in his eye! *Down ye go!*"

There was a yell, quickly curtailed, a splash, and then a long silence.

"Mrs. Brady, you are surely not holding that child under water all this time?"

But Mrs. Brady was already triumphantly applying the finishing touches.

"Now, there! Ye ain't hurt, are ye? Ain't ye nice an' warm? When ye go home, tell yer mother ye was swallowed by a whale. What! Ye *bad* little boy!"

The Infant had taken One-Two by the scruff of the neck, and had doused the unsuspecting cat in the water. One-Two came up sneezing and yowling in utter dismay. Hoo Chee leaned over and endeavored to scrub the cat as Mrs. Brady would have done.

A few minutes later there was a loud cry of joy. One-Two scampered at full speed along the hall, and

hid far under a lounge. Hoo Chee burst into the
room where Bayley was still fashioning the model.
The Infant glowed under a fresh and delightful sensation. He felt like dancing and singing, and presently
he broke forth:

Ah you wass — ah you wass?
Ah you wass — ah you wass?

And Miss Arenam laughed, because she thought the
child had learned from the streets a popular ditty that
asked:

How you was — how you was?

The Infant laughed too, and coquetted with the
lady, and would not let her touch him, but sought to
be pursued in fun. They chased each other about in
great glee, equally amused by the sport. At last Bayley caught him up, and kissed him soundly, and said:
"You darling child — I love you!"

And finally Mrs. Arenam found her daughter in the
arm-chair, with Hoo Chee fast asleep in her lap, while
One-Two dried himself in the sun, and tried to recall
just what had taken place in the tank-room.

THE amah had been revived, and had told her story
about the three men who tore the child from her arms.
Half an hour after Hoo King had returned with the
mother, he locked the women in the rooms, and de-
scended the stairs with the same expression on his
face that he had worn all day. He asked other tenants if they had seen the cat One-Two. The cat had
strayed away, said the father, and little Hoo Chee was

up-stairs weeping about it. Hoo King would give five
dollars for its return. He considered that any one
who knew about the cat would know about the boy;
for the two had been stolen together, said Kwee. They
had discovered that One-Two was a lucky animal, and
they would keep him alive and well. In time some
one would see the cat, even if the boy had been concealed or murdered. The father went to the various
haunts of his friends, and repeated his inquiry in a
careless manner. He went, also, to places where there
were enemies, and where he kept himself ready to be
attacked bodily. such were the relations of the Tongs
at that period in Chinatown. When he spoke, he scru-
tinized his hearers to see if they smiled wisely, or
otherwise betrayed knowledge of his greater loss.
But no one seemed even interested. There was nothing but to wait until the captors approached him for
a ransom. If he noised the truth, then perhaps the
hostile Tongs would find the child first and switch
him away. Nothing would please them better. They
could take Hoo Chee to Oregon, and keep him until he
had forgotten his parentage and had been developed
into a hater of his father's Tong. If the father told
the police, the newspapers would have it next morning. Besides, Hwah Kwee could give no clue to the
men; they had been too quick. He came home early,
in an evil mood. Hoo Bee had taken her lily feet to
bed, and was sound asleep.

It was the evening of the month when Miss Arenam entertained her little coterie of souls artistic.
While the Infant had slumbered above, the hours had

passed until the music-room was full of people, and
they had hushed to hear Miss Juliet sing while Dr.
Rimpo played an obbligato on the flute. In the middle of the song there came from aloft an inquiring
shriek of "Pay-ay-lee!" followed by the hurried pad-
ding of small, uncertain feet upon the stairs. Miss
Arenam blushed, and grasped the arm of her chair.
Hoo Chee, with One-Two tightly clasped under his
arm, dashed, shouting, into the room, then paused,
dazzled by the lights and the number of strange
faces. But Bayley, in her white dress, shone out from
all the rest like the main star of a coronet; and the
Infant, running joyously up, dropped on his knees before her and touched his forehead several times to the
floor. The music stopped: Dr. Rimpo had laughed
absurdly through his flute, and all the others joined;
for the soap of the bath had dried in Hoo Chee's cue,
which stood up as straight as the stem of a gourd.

All the ladies exclaimed:

"Where *did* you get that beautiful child?"

Miss Arenam told the story of the afternoon, while
the Infant examined all the people, and determined
that she was the loveliest.

"Now say the little piece," said Bayley.

"E-litty peesh?" repeated the Infant.

"About the little boy who was n't very bright."

Hoo Chee deposited One-Two carefully on the floor,
and, placing his hands on the lady's knee, looked
straight into her eyes and began:

> "Washee litty poy — washee baily plight-an
> Coutty tellee left flommy light-an;
> So-ey *shawdy*-dexy paw —"

2*

Here he stopped for breath —

> " — tilly *tinny* leddy law,
> To lemmemy latty lightee washee bite-an!"

Here the company broke into great applause, in which the Infant joined.

" ' If-itty-teshi-mow Jays," began the young person as soon as he could be heard; and he finished the lines without a break. There was more applause and laughter, and the ladies thronged to kiss the boy, while Bayley strove in vain to overcome the stiffness of his cue.

The song with the obbligato was begun afresh, and the evening went on with music. When Miss Arenam sang a Spanish ballad the Infant insisted on standing at her side, with One-Two under his arm, and staring up at her with open mouth, while his ears drank in her lovely voice. Next she sang the "Angel's Serenade," accompanied by the flute and violin. A strange sight then was the face of Hoo Chee. Never in his life had he heard anything like this. Perhaps he feared that Miss Arenam was only a dream and might vanish from him, leaving him to wake at the summons of the amah; for he clutched the lovely lady's dress, as if to stay her from moving, and then slowly the corners of his mouth drew down, and one, two, three came the tears in his upturned eyes, until they swam his sight away, and he stuck his little, hard pigtail into a fold of the angel's gown, and sobbed.

Thus again was the music interrupted.

"You darling child! What is the matter?" cried Bayley, taking him maternally in her arms.

"Bayley," said her mother, suddenly, "that child has not eaten a mouthful since he came to this house!"

"Oh, mama!" cried the girl, rushing off with him to the dining-room.

"How strange," said the mother, "that his parents have not inquired of the police, and been sent here!"

The Infant was left with Gee, who brought him a bowl of rice and some dainties prescribed by the lovely lady. Gee did not regard him with favor; for in their colloquy the boy had given him a "bad face" before the ladies of the house. Now, while Hoo Chee sat in a high chair at the vast table, much engrossed with filling a want which his previous excitement had made him ignore, Gee tried again to find out who he was. But the Infant had a very clearly defined purpose to conceal that much, and he answered most of the queries with the forgetfulness of a great capitalist on the witness-stand. At length the servant said in disgust:

"If you don't tell me your name, I'll whip you!"

"If you do, I'll call her," said Hoo Chee, with a small frown; "and she'll cut your head off!"

Gee made no attempt to carry out his threat, but instead went and whistled down to the basement. There was a galloping of claws and a sudden cocking of One-Two's ears. In a moment the cat's back arched into the most astonishing shape Hoo Chee had ever seen it take, and One-Two stood in a corner confronted by the small dog of the household. Prrout shared in the general surprise, and was half inclined to treat One-Two as an occurrence too interesting for malice. But Gee urged him on, and plainly indicated that the cat was an enemy to be destroyed. The Chinaman foresaw that the results might be disastrous to himself should the facts reach Miss Bayley; so he went discreetly below-stairs, where he found awaiting him his friend Lee Sing.

To resist showing Lee what sport was about to happen was too much for Gee's mood, and, grinning, he conducted his friend to where they could look through, and get a glimpse of the corner of the dining-room. One-Two, with bristling hair, was hunched in battle array, his eyes glaring into those of the enemy, who moved cautiously from side to side, wagging his tail in anxious respect for the cat's sharp claws. The Infant, whom the Chinamen could not see, had dropped his bowl, and stared upon the scene in the greatest wonder. In a moment he decided that his dear One-Two was in peril, and he immediately struggled down from the high chair to go to the rescue. Gee, hearing the noise, closed the door. He did not wish any Chinaman to know about the child; for if it was the son of a person hostile to Gee's Tong, then, no matter what happened, Gee would become the object of violence as the one responsible for an injury either effected or attempted. Only a Chinaman in Chinatown can understand.

"That cat is like one our Hoo King lost to-day," said Lee. "He offers five dollars for its return. It belongs to his little boy, Hoo Chee. Strange that a man should offer so much for a cat; but Hoo King makes money."

Gee received this information with a quickened mind. He was a member of Hoo King's Tong. He said nothing, but presently excused himself, and sent

Lee Sing on his way. Gee came half-way up the stairs and called:

" Hoo Chee!"

"What?" said the Infant, guilelessly.

The Chinaman laughed softly and retired. Then he slipped out, and ran over to the police station. There they telephoned to the Chinatown squad.

The Infant made straight for the dog.

"Go away, bad devil dog!" he said in Chinese, raising his small fists threateningly. Before Prrout had recovered from the novelty of this little figure Hoo Chee had snatched One-Two in his arms, and with difficulty had boosted him up to the high table. Then the Infant climbed back to his chair, where he leisurely finished his rice, stopping after each mouthful to let One-Two take his share from the bowl. Prrout after a while gave up his watch on them, and ran to find his mistress, who promptly sent him back to the basement.

Miss Arenam's evenings were always delightful. She was like California, thrilling and inspiring the charming people of many climes, and her guests invariably found the midnight come too soon. Now Mr. Paxton uncovered his new etching, and the talk having turned to art, Miss Arenam was persuaded to exhibit the unfinished bust of the Infant. It was placed in the front drawing-room, on a pedestal borrowed from one of the marbles, and the people thronged to admire it.

In the dining-room the small model, having eaten until One-Two refused to accept any more, and until he himself was compelled to desist with sighs, stuffed

much of what remained into the broad pocket that
ran across the breast of his bib. Then he got down
once more, and proceeded with lordly content to in-
spect this part of the premises. What a funny place
that was behind the screen — a long, low-opening in
the wall, with iron things, tipped, he thought, with
golden knobs, resting at its bottom on a level with
the floor, and, at the back, a wall of bricks built up
like stairs. Some day he could easily crawl in there
and climb up and see where it led to. How bright
and cheerful compared to the gloomy chambers on
Dupont street! And what a wilderness of curious
things! Those lights, fifty times as brilliant as the pea-
nut oil-wicks of home, how they dazzled one! They
— why, why — *this* was the House of Glittering
Things! And she — was the Lady of Cakes and
Tea! Why had he not thought? Oh, joy! This
was the goal for which he had set out — and oh, how
many, many weary miles he had walked! But he had
found it. He would stay here forever, and the Lady
would give him cakes and tea, and he would play and
play — where was little Quong Sam? Did Quong
have a One-Two? He would ask Gee. No; he would
run and find Pay-lee — she would be truthful.

A bell had rung, and Gee had gone through to the
front door. The Infant paused. In a moment he
heard a voice which sent a chill through his body.
It said in Chinese:

"Is a little boy — Hoo Chee — here?"

"Yes," said Gee. "If you will give me the reward
I will give you the cat, too."

Hoo Chee, standing behind the door with One-Two

in his arms, knew the voice as well as he knew the
color of his bib. Bayley came into the hall; he heard
her say things in English. He could not understand
them; but something in the tones made his heart
sink. Was he to be taken away from her — back to the
damp and darksome prison of three rooms? Never!

"There is a little lost Chinese boy here," said Bayley; "but how shall I be sure he belongs to you?"

Through Gee, Hoo King described his offspring.

"Yeh," said King, in answer to Mr. Arenam; "him
gottee one litty mole und' him chin, an' one litty mole
und' him ear."

"Let us examine the child," said Mr. Arenam.

Bayley went into the dining-room. Only the small
dog greeted her. Gee had left the door open. The
child was not to be found. They called his name, but
there was no reply. She sent Gee down to the servants' quarters, and went herself up-stairs, while the
guests peered under the furniture.

Hoo King grew uneasy. Perhaps this was a ruse
to gain time. He stepped in from the hall. Before
him on the pedestal was the cold head of his son — of
the color of clay. They had slain his only child!
There were no eyes; they had ground them up to
make photographs!

"What for! what for!" cried the wretched father,
laying his trembling hands on the pedestal, while his
knees nearly sank under him. He moaned many
words in Chinese. The searchers collected, thinking
the child had been found. Gee explained the cause of
the old man's grief, and tried to calm his fears. The
dog barked, and ran toward the dining-room, stopping

every moment and wagging his tail. Bayley hurried
distractedly for another look at the spot where she
had left the Infant. The dog danced about the fireplace, barking up the chimney in extravagant excitement. Miss Arenam heard the mewing of a cat.

"He cannot have climbed up there. Gee! Come
here!"

Gee inserted his head in the chimney space and received a kick in the nose from a small felt sole. Then
he drew forth a little shoe.

"Pay-lee!" implored the Infant from the dark
cavern.

Then One-Two and the defeated child were pulled
from the chimney, covered from head to foot with
soot. The Infant was weeping bitterly. The father
hurriedly grasped the cat.

"Ah!" he cried joyously. "It is one good-luck
cat!"

"Pay-*lee!*" beseeched the blackened child. He ran
to her with grimy, outstretched hands, his eyes quite
blind with tears.

"Your dress, my dear!" warned her mother.

But Bayley thought only of her unhappy little
guest. She quickly took him in her arms and kissed
his quivering mouth again and again. The contact
soiled the silk gown beyond repair.

The father rudely snatched his son away, and made
for the door.

"Pay-*lee!*" implored Hoo Chee, reaching out his
hands in vain. "Pay-a-lee!" Then he wept afresh,
as if his heart would break; and the street door closed
upon him.

"What a dreadful — dreadful shame!" said Miss Arenam, her eyes filling. "I — I don't think they treat him well at home. I —"

Then she went away to where they could not see her.

THE amah was asleep. Hoo King deposited the child on the mattress at her side. For most of the way Hoo Chee had hung listless in his arms.

"Go to sleep with your little cat," said the father, somewhat tenderly. "It is a good little cat, is it not?"

"Yes," sniffed Hoo Chee, slowly; "but — I wish —"

Then he was silent. The father retired to his room.

The child lay for a while staring up into the grim darkness, and heard the familiar spip-spop of the faucet in the sink. Then his mouth began to twitch, and he thought of the Lady of Cakes and Tea and the glorious House of Glittering Things. For a long time he cried softly to himself, while One-Two sat wondering.

Finally, the Infant's eyelids grew heavier and heavier, and his breathing less interrupted by sighs. At last sweet weariness came down and gently closed the big, brown eyes; and he forgot his troubles, and floated away, dreaming that he was a little fish in a pond with white porcelain banks, and was behind a stone, looking up out of the corners of his eyes at a tiny boy who held a cat.

THE CRUEL THOUSAND YEARS

HEN the grim ancestral joss of the Hoos led the family in an exit to a different domicile, the years of the Infant Hoo Chee were yet five. It was true that now he had the pride of silken strings to lengthen out his cue. But since the time when he had toddled away in pursuit of a lovely American girl, with whom he had wished to dwell forever in her home, which he called the House of Glittering Things, and since the moment when Hoo King had torn him from her whom the Infant called the Lady of Cakes and Tea, Hoo Chee had been more circumscribed than ever. Many a vision of that house and of that lady had been his as he seemed to be wistfully watching the humming world from the lofty flowerpot balcony. And no one but his meditative cat, One-Two, was solemn in the Infant's confidence, or knew the weight of his woe.

But on that day when the joss came down from the wall the few old smoky rooms were left as memories, and the father, Hoo King, and the mother and the amah walked away in the clear air, with Hoo Chee bearing the doubtful One-Two in his arms. Soon the Infant found himself in a second story, whence he

looked upon a yard impossibly great, he thought — a
yard as long as a cloud. It dissolved in the gloaming
as he gazed in awe, with his chin just over the window-sill, and he waked in the morning denying it.
But when he found it true, he rushed shouting down
the stairs, one step at a time, and shouting into its
vast freedom, where One-Two scampered in giddy
circles with his tail in mirthful curves. Here was a
roaming ground for all duration, and earth to dig,
and straggling weeds, and sticks and stones. It mat-
tered not what castles lay beyond; here was a park
that equaled the House of Glittering Things!

There was one restriction: he must never have aught
to do with the women who lived on the other side of
the fence, commanded Hoo King, for reasons of his
own. They were Sum Chow's women — Sum Chow,
who had the curio-shop, and opposed the traffic in
women slaves by the Tong which Hoo King ruled.
But women whom the Infant neither feared nor loved
did not concern him in his hours in the yard. The
marvel of his liberty filled his mind; it lost him his
appetite and some of his sleep for quite two days,
whereafter he ate like a knight returned, and slept as
hard as a horse can gallop, to be up and out, with
One-Two at his heels, catching the dew and the dawn.
In the other place on the balcony, never a smallest
finger might be laid on the stalk of a lily, nor a fea-
ther be drawn across one smooth green leaf, without
discovery; here, first of all, he pulled up a tuft of
grass, and saw its little white legs that walked in the
soil; and this was a secret in his bosom. Then behind the shed, which he called the Gruesome Go-

down, after the place where the doughty little Quong
Sam, of a story he knew, had been impounded by a
Sarcastic Turtle that stood between Quong Sam and
the House of Glittering Things; behind the Gruesome Go-down was a spot where One-Two suggested
by scratches that they dig, which they did.   The Infant made mountains and valleys with an iron spoon,
so clever he was, and he threw a pasteboard bridge
across a river-bed, and by it built an Important Town,
where the avenues were shaded by cabbage-leaf trees,
and where One-Two drilled wilful worms and rebel-
lious bugs as citizens.

From a window in Sum Chow's the learned Dr.
Wing Shee, that soothsayer whom all Chinatown respected, occasionally observed the Infant's serious
labors, and grew to like Hoo Chee.   The industry
which now was seen to thrive near the Important
Town was mining — in a pile of débris as high as the
Infant's self; and surely, in all the vast precincts of
the House of Glittering Things, no more absorbing,
dignifying occupation might be found!   With One-
Two's artful nasal divination they brought forth varied
bits of crockery that, when polished with One-Two's
ear, became as brilliant as other gems; and they drew
out many an odd fabric and buried relic that told of
bygone times and the domestic economies of extinct
houses.   The Infant could not stuff them all in the
pocket that ran across the chest of his bib.   The
choicest was a big green ring, like those the grown
folks wore, which the Infant squeezed as a love token
over the unwilling head of One-Two, who thence sat
apart, outwardly magnificent, but filled with supersti-

tious brooding. One-Two's splendor paraded the Infant's dreamland, and when in the morning he found that the mother had seized the bangle for her own bedizenment, a first black shadow fell across his shining new world. This was not like the House of Glittering Things. There the Lady of Cakes and Tea made peace and security for every one. He wished they would give him back his big green ring — just to play with; but they never would. He went and sat silently on his Important Town, with the corners of his mouth drawn down very far.

It was not like the House of Glittering Things, because here the days often promised happiness when they meant to end in sorrow. Once, while he played Bad Old Man with One-Two, there came a shower, and One-Two ran to shelter, shaking moist paws, to stand astounded at the antics of Hoo Chee. The Infant pranced with open mouth, delighting in the smart drops on his cheeks. It was superfine! And it was a headlong pitch from bliss to find himself pushed rudely into the house by his father. Up the stairs Hoo Chee must hurry, and Hoo Chee must stay to dry by the rice-pan-coals, while the rain made merry music, glistening and beating on the panes as if to ask why this little boy would not come out to play. And he wondered if the rain knew the Lovely Lady who had a deep, warm porcelain pond, and even urged people into it. Then the calm of another morning brought him the joy of a rusty pan a-brim with water, which must at once be made a lake for his Important Town; for the pan needed only a little fish to be perfect. But the little fish that after all day's strategy he managed to borrow from the amah's basket would not wag its tail and swim in the pan; and though he hid behind a corner and peeped ever so quickly out at it, still it floated disgracefully stiff on its side with its mouth stark wide. This would have been another bootless day; but the learned Dr. Wing Shee, who read your heart from your face as surely as he read the future from the stars, observed the Infant's listlessness, and came to the fence with a kindly smile. They talked of the wind and the sky, and the doctor promised to tell Hoo Chee some day the story of how the "Wretched Dragon Made the Sun Wobble."

"And I 'll tell you about the Sarcastic Turtle," said the Infant.

It was not wrong to talk to a man, and the women Hoo Chee had not seen. The women were Sum Fay —Sum Chow's wife, and their daughter, Sum Oo, whom a beautiful American patron had once addressed as Miss Oo, which had become Sum Oo's pet appellation.

THERE came love's month of May. The rains had ceased, and the skies were passing fair. The city lawns shone everywhere with summer plants; but Hoo King's yard was barren save of weeds. The learned Dr. Wing Shee, once looking over into the desolate space, threw a handful of seeds among the hills and valleys by the Important Town, where the cabbage-leaf trees lay pelted into the earth. Out of the doctor's privilege grew a garden for a child. The sun touched the place with magic, and the Infant saw with amazement his territory transformed. A morn-

3*

ing-glory shot out of the ground, and ran hand over
hand up a broomstick, shaking out its tender blooms
like banners. A beautiful yellow nasturtium raced
up following, and its blossoms bobbed in the breeze
to One-Two and Hoo Chee, as they stood and wondered at it. The Infant must march with exaggerated steps, singing:

Peely mow-wow — pilly willy *wop!*   *Peely* mow-wow — pilly
willy *wop!*

which were words of his own invention. In such
luxury of two kinds of flowers one imagined oneself in
a bower of the House of Glittering Things, with the
Lady of Cakes and Tea within call.

And the warm day arrived when the Infant, sitting
on the ground in speculation as to whether a Wretched
Dragon was as big as a cloud, heard a new sound. It
was a delicious sound. It was not a bird. It came from
the other side of the fence, — tones unlike any he had
heard, — and it kept saying, joyously and gurglingly
and fascinatingly, "Yai-yai-yah! Yai-yai-yah!" which
was clearly an expression of delight with all the world.
The Infant hastened to the fence. The merry "yai-
yai-yah" kept on with a relish of life in it impossible
except for one whose title to her big green ring endured unthreatened. The Infant forgot about whether
a Wretched Dragon was as large as a cloud or only
as large as some land, and he stood with his hands on
the fence, looking up at the tall boards that shut the
sweet sounds away. The tiny voice sang to itself and
talked to an older voice near by; all in the same
pleased syllables. At length it subsided to a con-

tented coo, and then it was still, and it did not come again. But it lingered in the Infant's ears like strange new music. At dusk he paused solemnly at the doorstep; he wished they might know that over here was a little Hoo Chee and his cat. But they were gone, and they would never know. Then, to his own astonishment, he dared to shout, "Yai-yai-yah!" whereupon he hastened up the stairs, frightened at his boldness.

He dreamed that the Sarcastic Turtle came and promised to let him stand on it to see over the fence. And the turtle crawled and crawled with the ever expectant Hoo Chee on its back, but the fence was always just so far away. And the turtle kept laughing and laughing, and bidding him rise on tiptoe, till the Infant awoke frowning, with his toes in tight bunches.

In the morning he and One-Two ran speedily into the yard; but it was too early for the little voice. All the brilliant forenoon he listened for it, as he pulled the shed hairs from One-Two's coat, and laid them one by one away in a little box; some one had said that the cat would need its hair again when the cold rains came. He would keep the box in the ginger-jar, where he hid his treasures now, and the ginger-jar should go in a secret place inside the Gruesome Go-down. Then, in the afternoon, and none too soon, he made a grand discovery. It was a knot-hole in the dividing-fence.

He looked upon a place where many flowers were, and the grass grew all of one height, like soldiers. And presently came out Sum Chow's young wife

bearing a mat. Behind her trotted a little dame of
scarce three summers carrying a fat cloth cat. It
was Miss Oo, and the Infant knew she was a girl, because she wore her tiny braids in two little horns that
were part of her spangled cap. The Infant saw the
mother leave Miss Oo to play alone upon the mat
that lay on the grass. These, then, were the women
of Sum Chow, who were to be avoided.

Miss Oo sat down and made remarks in her own
peculiar language to the fat cloth cat, and emphasized
them by shaking it up and down by the tail. Then
she rolled over and kicked her infinitesimal feet in the
air, and murmured demurely:

"Yai-yai!"

Her eyes traveled along the clear sky until they
met the sun. They looked without winking straight
into the glittering ball, in solemn satisfaction that
it should be there, and for a long time there was no
movement in her contented body but the occasional
wiggle of a raised and bangled foot cased in a silver-
trimmed slipper as big as an ear. The Infant stood
tight to the fence, fascinated beyond measure. In all
the adventures of little Quong Sam, from the beginning to the hero's arrival at the House of Glittering
Things, there was nothing so delectable as this! Now
it was occurring to Miss Oo that the sun made her
warm and happy, and that it was a good sun. A smile
began at her coal-black eyes, and ran down and tugged
at the curling corners of her ample mouth, until her
brown face was all aglee; and she kicked and laughed
and shook the fat cloth cat and shouted:

"Yai-yai-yah! Yai-yai-*yah!*"

Then she turned on her side, and in a few moments she had gone asleep with her thumb in her mouth, and the memory of the smile remaining on her round cheeks, while Hoo Chee and the cloth cat stared and stared and stared.

All the next day the Infant sought the fence at the slightest sound; but there were clouds, and Miss Oo came only when the sun invited. The clouds made him sad, and the day dragged like a faint headache. His night's slumber was invaded by a tiny maid carried in a splendid car, with all the background a gorgeous yellow blur of priests and gods. And the tiny maid shook a fat cat at Hoo Chee, and said, "Yai-yai-yah!" whereupon Hoo Chee stepped into the car with her. But just as they began to play Bad Old Man the car changed into tissue paper, and they fell through it and slid terrifically down the clouds, and the wee maid disappeared. And another night, just as a red toy-balloon was floating him over the fence, a Wretched Dragon, that was bigger than some land, gleefully gulped the balloon; and Hoo Chee and the tiny maid tugged and tugged at the string that hung from the Wretched Dragon's mouth—until it had a fit, and writhed and wriggled and shrieked so that the Sun Wobbled in the sky, whereupon the string broke, and Hoo Chee and the tiny maid sat down together very hard with the string in their hands, and he awoke to find her gone.

But the next day the clouds dissolved, and the sun sailed on as if nothing had occurred, and after he had tarried for hours by the fence he saw the procession of the mother and the mat and Miss Oo and the fat cloth cat. The Infant watched Miss Oo playing, and cooing, and rolling in the sun, till he wondered how it was that little Quong Sam had succeeded in crawling through the bamboo pole when he wanted to get on the other side of the wall; and Hoo Chee made a little sound with a stick on the fence. Miss Oo turned to listen, and when he knocked again she discovered the knot-hole. The Infant's heart gave a funny jump; she had stood up, and was coming to examine the fence.

" Little eye! " she said.

Whereupon Hoo Chee felt a hand upon him, and was whirled away from her sight.

" Go into the house, fool offspring! " exclaimed his father. " If you gossip with that girl again I'll keep you out of this yard for a thousand years! "

Hoo King pushed the stick through the knot-hole, and Miss Oo grasped it, unaware of the tragedy just enacted on the other side. When he drove it hard through, that it might not be withdrawn, a splinter caught in the small maid's finger. It did not hurt much, but she felt that something was wrong, and with her finger held up she trotted off to find her mother. Hoo Chee had gone with little steps into the house, with the corners of his mouth drawn down very far, hurrying as if something pursued him. A thousand years! The penalty was fearful even to think of, and it hovered around him for hours, like an oppressive spirit bound at last to drag him to despair. In a thousand years the Important Town would go to ruin, and lie at the mercy of the Monstrous Rat that lived in the Gruesome Go-down; in a

thousand years One-Two would tire of staying indoors, and would go away and seek the sun and the
fresh air and the fat cloth cat. And Hoo Chee would
gaze out of the window and see Miss Oo and the two
cats playing and playing and playing, and only once
perhaps in a hundred years would they remember
and look for Hoo Chee's mournful face behind the
pane. It was true that all this was only a threat, but
he felt it closing upon him as if it was real. He
wished he knew how to find the Lady of Cakes and
Tea.

He thought of it the next morning as he rummaged
in the Go-down, which first had stood so high in the
attractions of the yard, because it was doubtless owned
by the Monstrous Rat, with whom he had expected
many a sanguinary joust before he conquered it.
But now he had forgotten about the Rat. The dim
interior, piled with dusty crates and packing-boxes
long disused, was suited to his mood. Among the
empty boxes he had discovered a light one which he
could handle, and back of it he had found another,
much larger, into which by crawling a distance one
could squeeze and be quite out of the world. A loosened board on the side of the Go-down that fronted
on a strange yard let a shaft of sunlight into this re-
treat, and as he sat there he meditated breaking off
relations with his family, and abiding there permanently, to sally only at night. But a few minutes of
such life told him of its loneliness. He emerged, and
for want of occupation trundled the lighter box into
the yard.

How this box would have been used, if it had not

been for the awful threat, the Infant knew. Its awk-
ward dimensions would have been struggled with until it was finally mastered and made to stand against
the fence — so! And then it would have been easy
to bring that little fruit crate and hoist it on top — so!
After that it was baby's play to fetch these flower-
pots and fit them — so and so and so — one over the
other, till, boxes and all, they made a tower half as
high as the fence! It was an imposing structure,
hidden behind the Gruesome Go-down; and he wanted
to show himself how he would have climbed up on it
— if it had not been for the thousand years! All you
had to do, you see, was to step on the big box — so!
Then it was easy enough to reach the small box, and
you caught hold — like this — of the bit of frayed
rope nailed to the fence, and simply pulled yourself
up to the fence-top — like that; and — oh, dear —
there she was!

He stood breathless. Miss Oo lay asleep with her
thumb in her mouth, and the fat cloth cat lay in the
sitting attitude confirmed of fat cloth cats. A tall
calla lily bent and nodded its benison upon Miss Oo,
and her parted lips showed peeping teeth like rows of
little novices.

Suddenly she startled the Infant by opening her
eyes directly upon him. For an instant she caught
his full stare; but his glance fell away, and his tongue
searched the corners of his mouth. He dared not look
at her. Miss Oo began to smile.

"Little eye!" she said.

And the Infant twisted himself in such confusion
that he was in danger of falling from the flower-pots

into an ignominious heap in the middle of the Important Town. Miss Oo kept looking straight at him, and he would not meet her eyes, but looked quite over her and beyond, at space. She crawled some way, then rose and came toward the fence.

"Little boy?" she inquired.

Which so embarrassed the Infant that he sank down out of view, leaving nothing visible to Miss Oo but eight small grimy finger-tips on the fence-top. Womanlike, she made no effort to get him back, but waited in silence until the Infant began to wonder if she had gone, and he found courage to haul himself to see. She was there, sitting on the grass, absorbed in the finger-tips. At sight of him, the big smile came again.

"Miss Oo?" she said.

Which frightened him so that he sank down once more. But as he sat in cover, and heard nothing from Miss Oo, he was at length moved to say, but little above a whisper:

"Yai-yai!"

Whereupon Miss Oo responded with a giggle in her small voice, "Yai-yai-yah!" and the Infant could not refrain from calling back in louder tones, "Yai-yai-yah!" which Miss Oo repeated each time louder than the Infant, so that soon the merry contest of their voices had risen to such screams that it reached the ears of Hoo King. Hoo Chee's diffidence departed, and Miss Oo seemed charmed. When they were tired of shouting she searched her small collection of words. When Miss Oo liked people she talked to them.

"Rice cake?" she said, after a moment.

The Infant bethought him of the pocket of his

bib, and found therein a bean-meal cookie, which he promptly dropped into her lap. Miss Oo immediately began to devour it while Hoo Chee waited.

"Little girl?" he inquired at length in her own manner.

But she was too busy to answer. She looked at him over the cookie with two grave eyes, while the particles of bean-meal collected about her mouth. The Infant yearned for more conversation. He smiled engagingly and shouted "Yai-yai-*yah!*" and kicked the boards for her attention. But when Miss Oo looked up again she saw not even the eight grimy fingers. The flower-pots had given away, and the entire edifice of his love had fallen, bringing him to the ground in a mixture of boxes and broken clay. He had bumped his head, too, and his eyes filled with tears. Oh, if the Lovely Lady had been there he would have run to her and cried in the folds of her gown, and she would have comforted him, and taken him up in her arms? But instead he heard the voice of his father. He must not weep; he would need his tears. The thousand years were coming. He should never see the fence again, and there would n't be even a flower-pot balcony for him to come out on. His heart thumped against his ribs, and his pallor was evident even to his father.

But Hoo King did not suspect the gravity of the offense, and the penalty was merely that the boxes and the fragments all must be removed to the shed whence Hoo Chee had fetched them. The labor which had been lightened by novelty and by a magnetic attraction that had governed his will without a protest

now became an endless evil toil, and when it was
finished Hoo Chee was well nigh exhausted. Miss
Oo had long ago been taken into the house, explaining the crumbs of bean-meal on her face with the
words, "Little boy." The Infant went to sleep without a thought of supper, dreaming that he was an
executioner, and must keep chopping off a head that
forever flew up in the air and flew back, tight to its
body.

When he came into the yard once more he was in
no frame of mind to play Bad Old Man with One-
Two. How gloomy the yard was, anyway, thought
the Infant. It was a prison, where one might never
do what one liked most. Oh, if the Lady of Cakes
and Tea would but come and take him to the house
where all was light and freedom and peace! He went
off in a reverie of her, and of the wonderful porcelain
pond where, if one was not too frightened to search,
there were probably funny little wiggly fishes and
hoppity frogs. He was interrupted by the man who
peddled the flesh of the abalone, and who came through
the gate to interview Hoo King, whose wrath at being
disturbed sent the abalone man away, leaving the gate
ajar for revenge. The Infant saw the forbidden street,
and turned his back, for it invited him to run away.
With a weary spirit, he absently made pictures of rice-
cakes with a stick in the main street of his Important
Town.

The abalone man had gone to Sum Chow's and
seemed to be doing business there. The steps which
the Infant heard outside were not the abalone man's;
they were too light. It was some one coming into

Hoo Chee's yard — a woman probably — some woman humming to herself in a quiet way. The Infant scratched out the rice-cakes, and tried to make a picture of the golden fruit the Lady had given him. One-Two had gone to the gate. The small hum stopped, and the Infant heard a little voice :

" Yai-yai ? "

His heart beat in his throat. There she was. She stood, with a bright smile, well inside the gate, bearing the fat cloth cat. One-Two was sniffing the extraordinary phlegmatic creature with the stuffed tail, and Miss Oo was pausing for welcome. The Infant sat rooted with fear, giving no sign. Miss Oo waited but a moment; then she came and laid her hand upon his cheek.

" Miss Oo ? " she said.

The wee fingers were very soft, and the big black eyes looked straight at him in frankest liking. But the abalone man was coming, with his noisy cry. The father might think to have a glance at the yard — and it would mean a thousand years ! The Infant did not know how to make her go away. In his heart he wanted her to stay. The impulse to hide away with her came upon him like an instinct, and he took her hand and led her into the Gruesome Go-down.

He would crawl and show her into the packing-box ; she had followed him so trustfully. He picked his way over the flower-pots and behind the boxes to where he squeezed through the long and well-concealed passage to his cubbyhole, and Miss Oo, holding the fat cloth cat, followed at his heels as a matter of course. She crawled into the big box and arranged herself close beside him, while he eyed her with half-prevailing pleasure. One-Two sat before them gazing contemptuously at the fat cloth cat. Miss Oo looked about her and was deeply pleased.

"Little house?" she said sweetly.

Hoo King was outside. He went to the gate, then came back and looked for a moment into the shed, then went again to the gate. He called sternly to the abalone man across the street. Then Hoo King hammered at Sum Chow's open gate, and there was presently a hurried conversation half audible to the two in the cubbyhole. With one accord Miss Oo and the Infant remained silent, and in a short while the voices subsided and were forgotten.

The Infant found his precious ginger-jar, and he began to show his treasures — the many bits of colored crockery, and pins, and buttons and scraps of cloth, and every odd and end from the débris pile that had a brilliant hue or shape unusual. The small girl cooed, and reached for them as he silently handed them over one by one. Then he put them all back in the jug, where the box of One-Two's fur lay securely tied, and Miss Oo took the jar and rattled its contents, and threw it down, laughing at Hoo Chee's efforts not to lose the treasures when they scattered about the floor. Each time the good-natured Infant laboriously collected them all, the box of hair first, and each time the maiden rattled the jug and threw it down again. Miss Oo's attention was drawn from it only by a big cookie that dropped from Hoo Chee's bib.

"Little cake?" she said, holding out her hand.

He gave it to her, and received the ginger-jar in

4

return. She insisted that he take a bite with each of hers, and Hoo Chee, though he was not hungry, must accept when she stared at him and thrust the cookie under his nose. For him the cookie was not a success; it was almost like medicine. Conflicting emotions greatly disturbed him within, for all his pleasure in this lovely comrade. Now Miss Oo was busying herself with baring her feet of her tiny shoes, an act forbidden by her mother. Her glee at this quite drowned the Infant's trouble for a while. Hoo Chee must take his shoes off too, and it was hilarious fun to put them on Miss Oo's smaller feet, and see her giggle and kick them off against the ceiling of their little house. She became interested in her big toe, and brought it up to look at it. She began to frown: she could not remember its name.

"Little thumb?" she inquired doubtfully, staring at the wonderful member. But that did not seem right. In her perplexity she turned to Hoo Chee.

"Little nose?" she ventured.

"That 's your little big toe," said Hoo Chee; whereupon Miss Oo repeated the words after him, and went off into an ecstasy of laughter over her new knowledge. She shook the fat cloth cat by the tail, just as she had when he had seen her flirting with the sun. And Hoo Chee was so enchanted that he tried to shake One-Two by the tail. The young persons were severely startled by One-Two's instantaneous denial of this privilege. One-Two turned a somersault in the air, and sputtered and spun, and made expressions of most painful character, and disappeared in a rage that was really half jealousy. Then, in the narrowness of their little house, they began to lack new things to play with, and Miss Oo stared at Hoo Chee in expectancy.

"I'll tell you about the Sarcastic Turtle," said the Infant, finally, in an inspiration. "There was a man lost his head, and could n't find it anywhere — and was n't it too bad about the poor man? So he took some crutches and went to hunt it — so far that he wished he was home again. But the Sarcastic Turtle said, 'I'll take you across.' And when they got out in the middle the Sarcastic Turtle said, 'You must promise never to tell my secret when you get home. If you do I'll drown you right now!' And the man said: 'What is your secret?' And the Sarcastic Turtle said: 'Well, all the other turtles can say Yang-tse-kiang, but I can't!' And the man said—— but I'll tell you about a little boy," said the Infant, observing signs of failing interest in Miss Oo. She was sitting propped up in the corner, with her eyes half closed. She could n't follow the story; but it was pleasant to hear some one talk in a steady voice, when she felt as she did now.

"A Little Boy went out one day," said Hoo Chee, thoughtfully, "and followed her up the street. And she let him in, and it was the House of Glittering Things! It was all white inside, and there was plenty of cakes," said the Infant, whereupon Miss Oo opened her eyes suspiciously, "and it was lighted with stars and a dog and everything. And a man named Gee hated him, and went and told his father, and then he came and took me away from her; and I'll have his head cut off, and put it up the chimney, and then he

won't hate me any more! *She*'ll cut it off for me!
And then I'll stay in the house — and find little
Quong Sam — for a thousand years," finished the
Infant, abstractedly.

Miss Oo had gone to sleep. The Infant saw her
head rising and falling a tiny distance on her chubby
chest; but, lovely as she was, he wished she would go
home! He could not run to the house and leave her,
for the Monstrous Rat might come. It was wretchedly uncomfortable, for his father would surely be
seeking him. There she sat, with her hands hanging
at her sides like a Japanese doll's. He wished the
Lady of Cakes and Tea would appear, and take them
both away forever on a cloud that would float so high
that no one could reach it. He thought of the thousand years, and he was nearly ready to cry.

It was really a long time since they had entered the
Go-down. The learned Dr. Wing, pacing in Sum
Chow's yard, trying to reason out the disappearance
of two small children, became aware of faint sounds
coming from the direction of the Go-down, and after
listening carefully for a while to the story of a little
boy, laughed softly to himself and departed. There
were now people in the yard, the Infant knew —
several of them; and one was a man speaking Chinese
in a foreign accent. Then some one in a wonderfully
lovely voice spoke — a voice whose clear soft tones
penetrated the Go-down. Surely Hoo Chee had heard
that voice before! He grasped the ginger-jar and
crawled excitedly over Miss Oo's feet, and put his
head out to listen. O joy! and oh, most marvelous
surprise! It *was* the Lady of Cakes and Tea! He

wriggled out as fast as his hands and knees would
carry him, jostling the small maid, who murmured
sleepily, "Miss Oo?" and awoke to see his disappearing
heels.

Near the door of the Go-down the Infant paused
and peeped through a crack from behind a barrel.
He heard his angry father, who spoke but little English, hotly declaring in Chinese that when Hoo Chee
should be found he would be tied indoors—for a
thousand years.

"The fellow's a brute!" said the gentleman who
had come with Miss Bayley Arenam, in English.
"He still pretends to believe that you stole his boy,
and he threatens the child with torture — in the same
breath. If he is n't careful I 'll have the boy removed
to the mission."

"He *is* so dear!" said Miss Arenam. "You don't
think his father would hurt him, do you? I *do* hope
that some day I may do something to make Hoo Chee
happier!"

"I will teach him mission-school!" Hoo King was
threatening, while the Infant trembled and paled, and
scarcely felt Miss Oo behind him. "If he does n't
come home I will bring police to your house. And
there is one who can help me," said Hoo King, pointing to Sum Oo's father, who had just come hopefully
into the yard, after a long search through the quarter.

"Oh," said Miss Arenam, recognizing Sum Chow;
"is it your little girl who is missing — Miss Oo?
Surely no one would harm them! Do you think so?"

"Gone childs," said the learned Dr. Wing Shee,
appearing behind Chow. "Omens says shall be find;

4'

shall come from east," said the doctor, pointing toward the Go-down. "Omens say good times come for that poy, by by."

"She is good little girl," said Sum Chow, trying to smile. "She is too much — and the mother is too much sad. But we do not think you ——"

"Why don't the foreign devils go?" said Hoo King. "Why do they loiter on my premises? Do they want to steal me?"

The Infant shivered. He saw the Lovely Lady about to depart. She would disappear again — forever — and he would be left alone with his father. Ah, no, no! He rushed wildly out of the Go-down and after her, calling loudly:

"Ha-o, Pay-lee! Pay-lee!"

"Why, you darling!" cried Bayley Arenam, joyfully. "You were hiding?"

The Lady took the dusty young person up, and kissed him, and, as fast as she could, came trotting after him the barefooted Miss Oo, who ran to the Lovely Lady, and said demurely:

"Miss Oo?"

And when the Lady put him down, to look at the Infant and Miss Oo as they stood side by side, the Infant took hold of the Lady's gown, and turned his head back so that he could look beseechingly up into her eyes.

"We want to go home with you," he entreated, with frightened breath. "We want to go to the House of Glittering Things! We want to!" he begged, with a pain of suspense. "She'll be good, and I 'll be good. We don't want to stay here. We want to go home with you!"

And Miss Oo, hearing the Infant talk of going somewhere, decided that he should not suddenly forsake her again. She tightly grasped the tip of Hoo Chee's cue, and looked earnestly into the face of the Lovely Lady.

"The darling things! What does he say?" asked Miss Arenam.

"He says they want to go and live with you," translated Mr. Arroway.

"You angel!" cried the Lady of Cakes and Tea, kissing him again. "I *do* wish I could take you."

The Infant laughed aloud. It was all right, then! One could tell from the kiss and the tone, no matter if one knew not a word of what she said. He would go with her to the house — and the thousand years would be left behind! Hoo King was glaring at his son in a rage, but the presence of the gentleman who spoke Chinese restrained what the father might have said.

"Good-by," said Hoo Chee, radiantly turning his head to his father, but still holding tight to the Lady. "I go to the House of Glittering Things. I shall be always happy!"

"Ah!" cried Hoo King, beside himself. "Fool offspring! Fool! Come here; they have filled your impious body with devils!"

Hoo King made a dash for his son.

"No, no, no!" exclaimed Hoo Chee, fearfully, running behind Miss Arenam, with the troubled Miss Oo following after and holding to his pigtail. "No, no, no! Pay-lee! Pay-*lee!*"

But Mr. Arroway caught him.

"You belong to your father, little boy," he said tenderly, in Chinese, while Hoo Chee struggled and wept and hated him. "You must stay with him. I am sorry; but the Lady will come again some day — surely!"

Hoo King strode forward and snatched the Infant's hand, tearing his hold roughly from the Lady's skirt; and Sum Chow took the hand of his daughter. But Miss Oo began to sniffle, too, resisting with all her tiny strength the loosening of her grasp of Hoo Chee's pigtail. When it was accomplished she broke into a wail. "Miss Oo! Miss Oo!" she cried, woefully. Hoo Chee was dragged by his frowning sire toward the house, but the Infant wept no longer. His breath caught and caught, as if his bursting heart was forcing it all from his body; his brain was whirling in a panic. The sun was to be taken from the sky for a thousand bitter years.

Long after the yard was deserted there appeared at the window, just above the sill, a little round face with two red eyes and a mouth drawn down at the corners very far. A wind was sending in a swirling fog. The little red eyes overlooked the Important Town and the waving posies and the ginger-jar with the scattered treasures, and they saw into the empty Go-down. But those whose forms stayed pictured in his memory — Dr. Wing and Miss Oo and the Lovely Lady — they were gone — all gone — forever. They

were the only ones he loved, but he should never see
them again.   The wind slammed the gate and latched
it.   The little eyes blinked and blinked and filled till
they could not see; and the small head bowed on the
window-sill.

THE GENTLEMAN IN THE BARREL

THE GENTLEMAN IN THE BARREL

TRADITION says that the famous Wing Shee learned medicine in the street of the Thirty-four Sorrowful Grandfathers, Canton, from the tongues of the sacred storks whose eyelids he sewed together against the sight of happenings profane. Another tradition denies that he ever did learn it. Yet surely the doctor was a man of parts, and was gifted with every element, except the favor of chance, for what men call success. He looked frail in body; yet he had shone so valorous in the Taiping Rebellion that the mandarin in whose mob of militants Wing Shee marched had plotted perforce to extinguish him. Thus was Wing started on his wanderings, which stopped twenty years ago in a garret room at No. 13½ Beverly Place, San Francisco.

His walls were hung with water-colors reminiscent of screens and fans and china. There was a life-sized lady in much gilt embroidery, who walked due north, while her eyes yearned due south — a triumph of mind over matter. There was a beautiful flesh-tint of the fat Hoo King, who had refused to recognize it; whereupon Wing had given it the grimace of a fiend, and altered the eyes so that they looked at the nose.

For the doctor was public in any office of the brush. He would paint your face or a presentment of it, or he would paint your house. He would write letters, or big red visiting-cards, or signs. For a modest transfer he would chart an augury of all the delightful things to come in your career, forbearing mention of those miseries sufficient to the days thereof; and since it was done from seven random hairs plucked by yourself from your own head, there was hardly room for skepticism. But more than for anything else was he esteemed for his knowledge of diseases, and of how to make people think that they did not have them. He was unorthodox in this branch, as he was in others; and that, among the ignorant, has been ground for prejudice against him.

It happened that this little old gentleman, who was sixty-five, though you would have said fifty, found his room rent two months in arrears, with the prospect in one day more of being placed on the outside of No. 13½, with his pots, pans, and implements of art. Wing Shee, who had helped many a fellow in distress, and whose kindly eyes, through spectacles with rims as large as silver dollars, attracted every child, would have fallen into melancholy had that been possible to him; for his position seemed not to touch the hearts of his friends. The scholar's pride that kept him from meeting the issue by pawning the tools of his varied accomplishments they would have called presumptuous affectation.

About this time it became most important to the great Chee Kung Tong to know what mysterious business was done of nights in the rooms of the Tong styling itself the Ho Wang Company. The Ho Wang was ostensibly a corporation formed to deal in wines, and the twenty who assembled regularly in its rooms for secret deliberations, with some incidental good-fellowship and a little propitiation of the gods, were called the board of directors. Most men in China-town thought the machinery of the Ho Wang merely a blind against some foolish local law designed to dis-courage the lottery-gambler — an innocent person who chooses to do business by logarithms; or else they thought the twenty were manufacturing American silver dollars — a pursuit morally justified by the ever unsatisfied demand. But the great Chee Kung was anxious lest this might be the nucleus of a rival or-ganization growing out of the Chee Kung's despo-tism. A wall of the Ho Wang rooms was said to be inscribed with the names of its three hundred mem-bers. The Chee Kung wanted those names, and would pay for them.

Lung Tom and Hang Tow, the hulking day watch-dogs of the Ho Wang quarters, were not available. Lung Tom was successfully approached by a Chee Kung trusty, and said he was more than willing to turn an honest penny; but it was discovered that he could neither read nor write. Of Hang Tow the Chee Kung was chary, since he was suspected of being one of the Ho Wang's members. The two guards were never allowed in the rooms during the meetings, which lasted from eight o'clock at night until four in the morning; but all the rest of the time they were required to keep everybody out of the company's

premises, except the police, who were welcome. At
night either Lung Tom or Haug Tow was always at
the street entrance. The police used to come in once
in a while, at first; but they never discovered anything to warrant suspicion. The place contained a
number of wine-casks, an open fireplace with an iron
pot hung in it, and little else to attract attention. Religious ceremonies seemed the main diversion of the
Ho Wang.

One morning, at this juncture, two emissaries of
the Chee Kung climbed to the garret where lodged
the learned Wing Shee. They heard cheerful music,
and came upon the doctor curled in a small heap on
his divan, smoking a pipe and playing a mandolin.
Having conscientiously exhausted every project for
avoiding the ejector of tenants, and having failed, he
had turned to the companions of his leisure, leaving
the rest to fate. Fate entered his room in the persons
of the two from the Chee Kung. That a man reported
on the verge of bankruptcy should be thus passing
his time surrounded by numerous articles on which
money could be had at interest startled them. They
were men with paunches and other indications of
prosperity; but where they had expected to receive
deference they now bowed diplomatically low, and
proceeded in a subdued tone to lay their proposition
before him, while he graciously made tea, with no
sign of enthusiasm visible through the great horn
bows of his spectacles. When they had received their
cups and had seated themselves, rather awed by his
elegance of manner, the doctor said:

"What do you offer for this service? If I fail it
will be because I lose my life."

"What will you undertake it for?" asked the spokesman. The tea was excellent; the rumors about this learned gentleman must be ridiculously false.

"It will be one dollar for every name," said Wing Shee, rattling some keys in his pocket.

"Three hundred dollars!" said the spokesman. "Impossible! We will give you one hundred. No? Well, good morning."

The two retired slowly, as if expecting the suggestion of a compromise. Immediately the doctor jumped to the door. They had paused at the first landing below. He held the knob, ready to run and shout to them should they start down the remaining flights. But soon their steps were heard returning, whereupon he climbed briskly to the divan, resumed his pipe, and strummed a few chords on his mandolin.

"We have decided to accept your proposition," said the spokesman, "though as a member of the Chee Kung Tong, and as a man of means, we think you ought to do it for less."

"What can the Chee Kung do for me if I get a hatchet stroke in the nape of the neck?" asked the doctor, sweeping a wild discord over the strings. "Come back in thirty-six hours, and if you see me alive I shall ask you for the money."

The doctor played softly until they were gone. He reflected that a tenth of the sum would have tempted him. Meanwhile the spokesman of the Chee Kung was explaining to his companion that it is better to promise three hundred dollars than to pay one hundred.

When, later, the doctor returned from a visit to an American friend, he carried a box of tools, and up his

5

sleeve was a string of boiled sausages. In the hall a junkman had left an empty barrel so large that the doctor could barely get it through his door. It was strong and heavy, and had served perhaps in the vault of a vineyard. When he had locked himself in with it, he began to move about rapidly. On the divan he laid the sausages, some packages of drugs, his mandolin, his pipe and a supply of tobacco, a sharp knife with a case that looked like a closed fan, a bottle of ground Chinese ink with brushes, a bundle of long paraffin tapers, several books in his own language, and a bottle of rice gin.

Then Pow Lee, who kept the joss-house down-stairs, and occupied the other garret room, heard Wing hammering and sawing and planing. That pleased Pow Lee; for Wing, whose attitude toward joss-keepers was of small respect, was evidently forced to the wall, and must pack his belongings. The little man with the superior manner would have to take up his abode in some inferior lodging, where two others would sleep in his bunk during parts of the solar day. Pow Lee, who was growing wealthy as a member of the Ho Wang Company, could now rent this room for himself, which would suit certain financial plans of his not likely to mature under inspection.

At about dusk the sounds of carpentering came but intermittently; and when Pow Lee, after no answer to his knock, peeped curiously in, he found no one. That seemed strange, since he was sure he had heard a hammer-stroke but a minute before. A blue barrel lay in a pile of shavings. Pow rolled it, and found it heavy; it was surprising that Wing could have

filled a barrel and so little changed the aspect of the
place. A medicine-box was on the divan, an opportunity welcome to the inquisitive joss-keeper. But
when he touched it there came from near by the sharp
sweep of chords on a mandolin. It was evidently
Wing returning. Pow Lee fled.

Lights began to shine from the house. The blue
barrel lay in the twilight. Occasionally it oscillated
gently, as if some heavy person had run across an ad-
joining room in the flimsy building. A cloud of
tobacco smoke hung closely around it, as though
brought from the ceiling by a mood of the atmosphere. By and by an American in a leathern apron
came with ropes and let it down the stairs. Then he
locked the door and took the key. At the street the
barrel escaped from the ropes and trundundled across
the sidewalk, where it stopped abruptly against the
wheel of a wagon. The man with the rope apologized, though it was not plain to whom.

Later, in the back room of the Ho Wang Company,
Hang Tow drowsily opened his eyes and then went
to sleep again, while Lung Tom ranged in line some
newly delivered casks. The blue barrel had arrived
among them; and this he left upright at one side
of the room. Once, while Hang slumbered, Lung
moved it a foot or two.

When Hang awoke he saw Lung sitting on the blue
barrel, gazing toward the wall at a long line of hiero-
glyphic names he could not read. Before long the
Ho Wang would be assembling. Hang lumbered
with interest over to the barrel that was different
from the others.

"It does n't belong here," said Lung. "The man came back while you slept, and said he would call for it in the morning."

"Unusual barrel — has two bungs! Wonder what's in it?" said Hang, with pregnant curiosity. But Lung did not seem to care. Hang could hear no swish of liquids; its contents were evidently solid, since they made a sound when Hang turned it upside down, which was quick work for a man of his strength. At each end at regular intervals there were small round holes in the staves, but the holes had been closed from within. It worried Hang why, if the contents were not valuable, this had been done, and new heads put in. It occurred to him that between four and six in the morning he might be able to open the barrel; and should he take a fancy to anything in it, he could lay the blame on the honest Lung Tom, to whom the American would naturally look should anything be missing.

"Time!" called Hang at length to Lung, who appeared to have started a nap. "The chief said he would discharge you if he found you asleep again."

"He told me," said Lung, without opening his eyes, "that if you did n't smoke less opium he would discharge you."

Before they left for the front room Lung rolled the barrel to a far corner. It oscillated to and fro several times, and finally, with an unnatural lurch, came to rest. A vapor like the smoke of tobacco began to rise from its vicinity; but the air was so Chinese, and the room so dimly lighted by a single oil lamp, that no one would have detected this phenomenon.

At eight o'clock Hoo King, the chief of the Ho Wangs, arrived with several members. Hang Tow had hastened to supper, whence he would seek his favorite opium-joint, where they never failed to drag him from his stupor at exactly half-past three in the morning. Lung Tom told Hoo King about the blue barrel, and took up his station at the street entrance to the hallway.

The members stopped in the front room, where there were chairs and gaslight. From the dim corner of the back room, where the barrel lay on its side, it was possible to distinguish only that a business meeting was being held. At first any one who opened the communicating door might have heard, from a source hard to say, the tinkling of a mandolin, apparently distant, and surely in the hands of a master. But soon the music ceased.

Two hours later Hoo King led the way back for the serious work of the night. He and those who thronged after him were all well known in Chinatown. Hoo King was a ginseng merchant and a general manipulator of profits; Ma Tee owned a factory which supplied cigars to all men who could not afford good ones; the fat Fong Ah was proprietor of a washhouse in which labored eighteen less fortunate Chinese; Fai Chu was known to every man who had been sick, for he sold drugs in one of the neatest shops of the quarter; Lee Yip was president of a curio-shop much patronized by tourists; Fuey Ying slaughtered pork, and found a market for nearly every pound of it among the Celestials; Pow Lee sold joss-sticks, and

ate the offerings to the gods; Hai Lo was head spirit
in a mysterious place called the Hole-in-the-Ground;
and there were twelve others, all of fresh-shaven heads,
and portliness, and clean clothing in noticeable col-
ors. They wore red buttons in their caps, and their
trousers were tightly wrapped at the ankles. Their
dignity and the tobacco they smoked belonged to a
prosperity hard to explain.

Hoo King, who was telling Ma Tee about the blue
barrel, said suddenly:

"The idiot — he told me he put it in the far
corner!"

The blue barrel was standing upright in the center
of the room.

When the heavy shutters of the rear windows had
been barred and the door locked, and the chief had
wrapped around his wrist the end of a fine wire that
hung from the ceiling, four casks were brought forward and their bungs drawn. One after another each
of those present took from his sleeve a bag, from
which he counted twenty double eagles, holding every
coin so that all could see it, then dropping it into one
of the casks. When the money had been equally divided among the casks the bungs were replaced, and
there began a very long process of rolling the casks
to and fro across the floor. Every few minutes new
sets of men came forward for the work, which was
arduous enough to set beads of perspiration on the
faces of the fat Fong Ah and his counterpart Fuey
Ying.

It was well past midnight, and the rolling was nearly
at an end, when without warning Hoo King's hand

flew up, jerked by the wire attached to his wrist. He shouted a word of gibberish, and, freeing himself, dropped cross-legged in the middle of the room, breaking into a chant like those of the Taoist priests. Quickly six others joined him, and one man began pounding a gong while another played on a squealing pipe. The transformation was creditable from a dramatic point of view; the noise was deafening.

The door swung easily open, and admitted a sergeant of police, followed by a party of tourists and a Chinese interpreter.

"Shut up!" shouted the sergeant, crashing his stick on the panel. "Now, you, John, tell the ladies what kind of a fandango this is."

"This," said the interpreter to the ladies, "is a new kind of leligion — baily diff'unt than all other kinds leligions of China. All those make-to-write on that wall was petitions to Heaven. Those men wusship one big yellow god named Yangtse — baily much same all you 'Melicans wusship."

"Well," said a lady, "they are started in the right direction. Who knows but that they will finish by becoming Christians?"

"More likely to finish in jail, ma'am," said the sergeant, who had had experiences. "This ain't much. But now I'll show you the old woman who sells live cats' eyes."

The party filed out, each lady with her skirts in one hand, and her smelling-bottle in the other, the men puffing at cigars in competition with the air of the place.

Then the scene changed back. The contents of the

casks — water, sand, and coin — were discharged, and
the money was restored to its owners. The opera-
tion was Hoo King's method of "sweating" United
States gold coin, the result of his many years of experience. Hoo King was the man who knew the right
quality of sand, and judged the coins, and controlled
the best methods of disposing of them after they had
been robbed of enough metal for profit. The water
with which the sand had been washed was placed in
a big kettle to evaporate, and while the fire roared
beneath it the members sat smoking, and whiling
away the time with jovial conversation. Those who
had to be up early stretched out in sleep.

When Pow Lee recognized the blue barrel, and
stated positively where he had seen it a few hours
before, it came in for much attention and gossip.
There was a general feeling of pleasure in this group of
men opposed to the learned Wing Shee both morally
and mentally, over the proof of the financial straits
into which he had fallen. Fai Chu disparaged him as
a quack who had been the death of countless patients.
Hoo King spoke of the rejected portrait, which in its
altered form was a constant thorn in his side, and
suggested how agreeable it would be to roast the doctor in his own blue barrel over such an excellent fire.
Pow Lee seconded their sentiments with spirit, and
searched for the ax, proposing that the barrel be
broken in and its contents examined. With his own
eyes, he said, he had seen Wing Shee packing in it
the cross-eyed portrait of the chief of the Ho Wang,
together with many strange dried animals such as
Wing ground for his magic medicines. Here was a

most desirable opportunity to get possession of the portrait, and examine the outlandish beasts at leisure. The doctor's false pretenses could be exposed. The others hammered the barrel, and rolled it, and turned it upside down.

"Look out!" said Pow, coming up with the ax, "Just let me have one blow!"

But the fat Fong Ah stayed the arm of the joss-keeper.

"It won't do," he said; "for if the white man who brought it makes complaint, the police will search this place too thoroughly."

When four o'clock arrived, there had been a brief process with crucible and bellows, and the directors of the Ho Wang Company had gone home to peaceful slumber.

At this point enters something like a question of veracity. Hang Tow returned rather heavy with opium, and saw the blue barrel lying on its side. The two watchmen lay down in different corners of the room. Each insists that he slept until seven in the morning without a break. Hang says he had a dream. Their statements are improbable.

Hang's alleged dream was that he awoke and heard a sound as if one of the casks was being rolled very slowly across the floor. There was a mild collision with another cask, and then a silence that caused a rising of his loose scalp-locks. Soon came more of this cautious rolling, and another bump, after which he presently saw in the direction whence proceeded the noise eight tiny points of light gleaming in the darkness a few feet above the floor. The lights shone steadily, and there was no further sound. This phenomenon filled Hang with a contest of fear and curiosity, in which the latter finally prevailed, so that he crept gently toward the lights. When he was nearly within reach they disappeared. He struck a match, and confronted the blue barrel.

If the luminous glances of one of Wing's diabolical animals had made the glimmer, the monster was probably too big to escape and be at him from the bung of the barrel. He lighted the lamp, and with the handle of the ax knocked in one of the two bungs. It is absurd to assert that this action would not have aroused Lung Tom. Hang tried to see into the barrel, but his head got persistently in the way of the rays of the lamp. He went around and knocked in the other bung, so that the light might shine from the other side. But as soon as he left the first bung-hole for the second, the first bung was replaced from the inside of the barrel! He could not run around the barrel quickly enough to get ahead of the demon imprisoned within.

But now he wedged a broomstick firmly between two other casks, so that its end went a short way through one of the bung-holes and prevented its plug from being put back; then once more he thrust in the second bung. Now he could see! His eyes met two large shining disks like spectacles. That was all.

There came a puff as from some one blowing dust, and a cloud of blinding, stinging red powder filled his eyes, putting out his sight, and causing him to howl with pain. As Hang Tow raised his hands to his

brow, the barrel lifted from where it stood, and fell
heavily upon his nose, throwing him on his back.
It rolled off with a thunder that would have awakened
ten Lung Toms. But Lung made no sign. It is not
known just what further harm the barrel did to Hang
Tow, but when it had finished with him it waddled
up to the lamp, blew out the flame, lighted a taper
inside of itself, and settled down comfortably.

When, late in the morning, Hang awoke and saw
Lung sitting in abstraction on a cask near by, Hang
gazed inquiringly through red and tearful eyes at his
honest fellow-watchman. Lung Tom glanced at him
without emotion, and said simply:

"Too much opium."

The blue barrel was gone.

SNUBBY TAGGERTY had the barrel in hand. It was
he who had carried and brought it. He was talking
to it while he urged it through the door of the garret
in Beverly Place. When he had locked himself into
the room, and had said, with a sigh of rest, "All
right!" two flaps opened in the head of the barrel,
and Doctor Wing Shee looked again upon his beloved
abode. His head was swathed like a Moslem's, and
his cue was coiled into an additional buffer at the
top of it.

"You pullee me," he requested, with a feeble
grimace.

Taggerty, who was not very tall, stood on a chair,
and tried to extract the learned gentleman from
within. But the doctor's legs, cramped by eighteen
hours in one position, refused to turn on their hinges,

and his knees caught provokingly against the fixed part of the barrel-head.

"Hol' on, doc," said Taggerty, suddenly releasing his hold, and letting his friend slump back to the interior of the barrel. "Wait till I t'row it over."

When the barrel was on its side, Taggerty slowly manipulated the body of his friend as he had sometimes worked large bedsteads through narrow doors, and finally produced him complete on the floor. The doctor smiled in the best of humor; but when Taggerty took him under the arms and raised him to his feet, the old gentleman's legs refused to straighten, and he flopped back to a cross-legged position in the pile of shavings.

"Too muchee same, allee time," explained the doctor, cheerily, while his friend placed him on a chair, and tried to pull his legs in line. "No; you go that closet — look shee black bottle."

Taggerty drew forth a jar of whisky in which floated the remains of a plucked fowl.

"What the dickens is the birdie, doc?" said he, in wonder.

"That him cloe-bud; make 'Caw, caw, caw!' You sabbee? Baily good for no-can-walk."

Half an hour's rubbing with this liniment left the Chinaman fairly restored, and not long afterwards the two deputies of the Chee Kung Tong, climbing the garret stairs, heard the familiar tinkle of the learned gentleman's mandolin. But this time when they came in they found Snubby Taggerty with him.

"Here is a book with 303 names of the members of the Ho Wang Company, as written on the walls of its rear apartment," said the doctor, leaning over the blue barrel. "Three hundred dollars, however, will be sufficient."

The visitors exchanged glances.

"We 'll give you two hundred," exclaimed the spokesman.

" *Three* hundred dollars will be sufficient," said the doctor, in a tone full of meaning.

"But how do we know they are genuine? Besides, if you don't accept our terms your trouble will have been for nothing."

"You accepted my terms yesterday. My reputation guarantees their authenticity. As for the rest, it will be more profitable to me to drop the book into this barrel, in which there is an inch of coal oil. With this taper," said the doctor, lighting it, "I can fire the oil, and destroy the book of names — the valuable book of names — instantaneously. I give you a minute by my friend's watch to decide. You look shee," said the doctor, in English, to Taggerty.

The envoys departed, leaving Wing Shee in possession of fifteen big gold pieces.

The door had barely closed before it was opened unceremoniously by a creature with a hooked nose and a mouth of disdain, who said to Wing Shee briefly:

"Well, to-day is the thirty-first. What is it — pay or get bounced?"

"Say, feller," said Taggerty, who sat easily in a chair, "that ain't the way to speak to a gent like this. He 's first cousin to the King of the Asiatic empire, he is — an' I don't like yer ugly face, savez?"

"What have you got to do with it, you snub-nose?" said the ejector of tenants, scornfully.

"Oh, let 's see!" said Taggart, joyfully. "Count

'em out, doc; an' see he don't cheat on the change. Did n't I tell yer the doc was in the swim? I 'm his chief bull-whacker, I am — take a run!"

The ejector was rudely ejected by the collar, and from the stairs were heard sounds of a person descending with great difficulty, but with much haste.

"Say, doc," said Snubby Taggerty, when he returned, "was they really three hundred members to that outfit?"

"Oh, no," said Wing Shee. "All those names dead men. They was put on that wall to make foolee people. But you baily good boy. I give you twenty dollies."

"Naw! You 'n me 's even for the time you fixed me busted eye. But they 's twenty live ones, anyhow. An' you 'n me 'll get a *reward* from the Gov'-ment for nosin' a counterfeiters' nest. Say, I 've got a scheme or two to let you in on; for you 're a dandy — you are!" said Taggerty, gazing admiringly at the blue barrel. "Bye!"

After a while nothing remained of the blue barrel but a pile of kindling-wood. The learned Doctor Wing Shee sat on his divan, playing the mandolin softly, and now and then taking a whiff from his pipe.

"The best of it," he said to himself, with a quiet smile, as he stared through his great spectacles, and thought of the time he had spent in the barrel reading by the light of a taper, "is that, after twenty years, I at last finished the 'Story of How Yuen Liu Taught the Stork to Play Shuttle-Cock,' which, to me, is the most stupid and improbable of the Seven Thousand Classics."

THE MAN WHO LOST HIS HEAD

IX Chinamen were climbing Jackson street, in San Francisco. They were men who bent for thirteen hours a day over the laundry benches of the fat Fong Ah, which lie out of Chinatown. It was after midnight, and the wooden walk was deserted and fairly wide; yet they marched dispersed in Chinese file, as if they were still worming the narrow, crowded thoroughfares of their city of Canton.

Their conversation was like the gargling of mixed consonants; and their garments were as made for one man from one pattern. Of all concerning them what was most civilized was the cold, hard look on the face of the hindermost one — Ah Koo. Ah Koo was silent. While all the rest discussed the theater they had left, every man staring straight in front of him as if soliloquizing aloud,— while all the others were loquacious, Ah Koo seemed sullen. Often he glanced back, especially when he heard footsteps behind. When presently they had left the Celestial quarter well in the rear and had turned into the street where the Fong Ah laundry is, Ah Koo suddenly darted into the dark shadow of a doorway, and the others, on their felt soles, noiselessly and without missing him, vanished from sight.

Now in this, as in many things, were women involved; and they were two — Loo Kee, who toddled
through life, and Fah Now, who shuffled.   Loo Ning
was their lord, an importer of sea-cabbage and odd
vegetables, who dwelt in a suite of rooms over some
stores on Dupont street. He had ebony tables. When
the wind blew holes through the bright paper lanterns
that bobbed from his balcony he hung out fresh ones,
which means that he was prosperous.   Loo Kee toddled through life because her feet had been tightly
swathed in silken bandages from the time she was six
years old until she was twelve, so that now she could
walk but with the help of the normal-footed Fah Now
— the minor wife — who wore slippers that flapped
with every step she took, because they had no heels
and were kept on only by a big toe pointing upwards.
Fah Now had no greater charm than her face; but
Loo Kee had sat on a daïs six years, outgrowing her
feet, and had then learned many arts and graces,
especially arts.

That daïs period had been in Canton, and its end
came when they told her parents that a wealthy Chinese, gone abroad, besought her to wed. The parents,
jingling a thousand Haikwan taels in their pocket,
which was in the trousers of her father, accepted the
sum as a proof of the gentleman's love; and they
stuffed little Kee with stories of splendor and silver
castles awaiting over the sea; and then stuffed her
into the steerage of a giant craft where for three long
weeks they fed her occasionally and watched her unceasingly. And when she was landed and dragged
successfully past the mildly inquisitive revenue flag

of the United States her value to Loo Ning, who had
imported her, was estimated by him at fifteen hundred Haikwan taels, net.   To the rescue society Loo
Ning solemnly swore the affair was romantic, that she
had been betrothed to him since her youth.   And little Kee, as she had been primed for it, swore the same.
What puzzled people who saw this sort of thing for
the first time was the phrase "since her youth," for
her youth was barely begun.

Up to then Loo Ning had been in America twenty
years.   But a previous thirty years had been spent in
Canton.   There, strangely, his name had been, not
Loo Ning, but something else, and he had practised
appropriation all through the Kwangtung province.
The officers of the government, who believed that
they stole everything unchained in the Middle Kingdom, grew a professional jealousy of him, such that
there came a dispute between him and them concerning his life, they and he craving it for incompatible
uses.   And a man with a sword ran miles in pursuit
while Loo Ning fled along the banks of the Canton
river — a curious case of two persons impelled in the
same direction by opposite sentiments.   A few weeks
later the sword and Loo Ning turned up in Hong-
Kong, and from that English port, whence in those
days there was no extradition, it was easy to ascend
to the Golden Gate.

But these were his bottom days, and afterward he
prospered.   In the course of his rise he took to his
household the handsome Fah Now, aforesaid, she big
of foot, soft of heart, and worth half a thousand dollars to her parents.   Then he grew richer and sent

for Loo Kee, and made Fah Now but a tirewoman to
her.   Fah Now's face was pleasanter to see than Loo
Kee's, but you looked at their feet.

Ah Koo was Loo Ning's nearest of kin in America,
employed by Loo Ning's friend, Fong Ah, and thus
came often to see Loo Ning.   And the beginning is
that Fah Now, the forsaken, began to yearn for the
admiration of Ah and for human sympathy.   The
lady, Loo Kee, too, welcomed Ah always with smiles
that should have caused Fah Now anxiety.   But Fah
Now was simple, and as yet what Loo Kee thought of
Ah Koo or what Ah Koo thought of either woman
was unknown to Fah Now.   Loo Ning was jealous of
both the women in the ratio of five to fifteen.

One evening Loo Ning had been called to preside
at a dinner where various secret affairs were adjusted
and many a bottle thatched with straw was found to
be all right.   Ah Koo thought that Loo Ning might
return full drowsy with *hak-tow-shu*, which is dark
brown gin, and might thus lie low in a stupor, leaving the women less embarrassed than they were in the
sober presence of their watchful lord.   In this hope
Ah withdrew near midnight from the fan-tan game
at the place called in Chinese the Hole-in-the-ground,
and issued demurely from one of the dozen escapes
from that subterranean temple of Chance, and walked
a little away and climbed the dingy stairs to the splendid odor of opium, sandal wood, and leeks that clung
to Loo Ning's aristocratic abode.   Ah came stealthily
and listened at Loo Ning's door and discovered that
Loo had come home from the dinner, but charged
with *hak-tow-shu* only enough to arouse his strongest

proclivity. There was a family jar; Loo Ning was
bawling insults to the lady Loo Kee, who sat mute
and fearing violence. The child, Loo Wah, was
rushing around to be out of the way as his father
strode up and down kicking the furniture and assert-
ing that Ah Koo had been meeting with favor from
Loo Kee, and should perish for it. Loo Kee should
be sold to the highest bidder, promised Loo Ning, and
with that he kicked a box of toys from Loo Wah's
hands and scattered them over the room.

That frightened the child, who, conceiving his
father's effort as hostile, fled to the hall like a flying
squirrel, all yellow sleeves. Young Loo Wah slammed
the door so that Ah was not seen standing outside,
surprised by the light that flashed in his eyes. The
matter served as pretext for trembling Fah Now, who
had all the while expected her mistress to fasten on
her the blame of a new jade earring found on the
lady's lacquer tray, and not the gift of her lord. Fah
Now therefore went after the child and brushed by
Ah Koo, who was flat to the wall in the shadow. The
sounds within lessened and finally ceased, for Loo
Ning was content and had taken his pipe with the
long, slim walking-stick stem and the bowl of an
acorn's size. In the darkness without the roughly
dressed little Fah Now felt her garments plucked and
knew well the voice that whispered her name. Ah
put his hand on her shoulder and urged her to guile
with the master, such that Kee might bear the weight
of the gaud which he said he had left in the tray for
Fah Now alone. The big-foot woman readily fell to
his pleading, and breathed a sigh, wishing with all

6*

her foolish heart that he could steal her away from
her master. Ah understood and made haste (this
being the first interview he had obtained with her
away from the rest) to say that he intended some day
to purchase both her and the lady Kee from Loo Ning
— which no laundryman ever could do who worked
at Fong Ah's wages, and that to please Fah Now the
small-foot Loo Kee should be made a servant and
tirewoman to Fah Now, instead of Fah Now's tend-
ing as then to the wants of Loo Kee. The foolish
big-hearted Fah Now laughed with delight. Then
the door opened, and in the full glimmer of the oil
lamps they stood before Loo Ning himself, his face
transfixed with rage and astonishment.

Fah Now whirled from the spasmodic clutch of Ah
Koo and dashed from her slippers, becoming a ghost
of white stockings in the dark up-stairs. Ah sprang
back for defense, but Ning had turned for a weapon
that hung on the wall. The weapon was a little fan,
with twin knives concealed within it. Ah took flight
down the stairs. Ning then stopped, to provide himself with another weapon.

It was not the late returning crowds, nor that two
policemen of the Squad stood near, that prevented
Ning from pursuing Ah when Ning reached the street
a short distance behind him. Ning could have used
the hatchet in his sleeve to cleave Ah's skull, and then
could have jumped down any cellar-way and burrowed
for a block underground, or run to the roofs and gal-
loped over the pickets and barbed-wire fences dividing
them to a dozen places of safety, where both friends
and foes would have secreted him from American

law. But Providence sent the procession of Ah Koo's
five fellow laundrymen passing the door as Ah reached
the street; and Ning knew they would stand by Ah
to a man. Ah dropped into step with the others, and
soon understood that Ning would not attack him at
once. Ning fell far behind, but Ah Koo climbed
Jackson street in a sullen mood. His companions
were accustomed to this, and suspected nothing.

When Ah, unknown to the rest, had silently turned
into the shadow of the doorway, he smiled with a new
idea. The streets were still and the moon was low.
The gas lamps had not been lighted, and after moon-
set that part of town would be left in darkness. The
time passed slowly. A man and his wife came quar-
reling home. Their voices echoed against the walls
of the houses, and Ah muttered words of disgust at a
system that loosens the tongues of women. A fellow
in liquor scared the Chinese with a feint toward the
door-step, and then started back, frightened at Ah.
Finally, with his sleeves joined together in front as if
his hands were cold, Loo Ning rounded the corner,
staring impassively before him, like an automaton in
yellow wax. He walked by Ah Koo, and then along
and down behind a rise in the street, still gazing
stolidly into the fog that now crawled over the hills
from the Golden Gate. Ah Koo arose from the shadow
and started back to Chinatown.

The women had put out their lights, but they did
not retire. Perhaps they both would be beaten when
Loo Ning returned, and it was better to be thickly
dressed. The youthful Loo Wah, induced to come

out of the gloom by many asseverations that his father had gone, sought refuge in sleep and lay on a mat, bare of foot and clothed as he was — by the preoccupation of the tearful Fah Now, who settled herself in the dark near by. She would not be surprised if she met death before morning, yet was fearful for what might happen to Ah Koo.

The young Loo Wah turned on his face and snored. The woman heard footsteps outside and held her breath. Loo Kee was in another room. Some one slowly opened the door, stepping lightly as Chinamen do. She thought it was Loo Ning, returned with the truth and bent on violence; and when she was touched she shrank with a shudder. But she heard the false voice of Ah Koo, whispering something which she believed because she trusted him.

"I have killed Loo Ning!"

Fah Now jumped to her feet and would have made an exclamation; but Ah commanded her to be dumb, and she obeyed with the precision of Chinese women when they love. He pushed her into a chair, and she let him bind her hands with a cord, believing it a detail of some plan he had formed for taking her off with him. When he pulled it too tight into her wrists she trembled, but made no sound. Then he tied her feet to the rung of the chair, so that she could not have moved except on her knees, with the chair on her back. The only light was a little flame waving before the joss in a case on the wall, and she could not see by it the expression on his face. She felt reassured when he sat alongside and said:

"Do you like me?"

The woman opened ready lips to speak, and instantly the thick braid of her hair was drawn across her mouth between her teeth, and Ah hauled it so taut that it strained at the roots, and he tied it fast with a hitch at the back of her neck. Fah Now could neither speak nor walk. She was surprised to hear him lock the door and grope toward another that led to Loo Kee's sitting-room, where Loo Kee waited in desperation for what her lord might do.

When Ah lighted the wick in Loo Kee's oil cup she started up, and asked:

"Loo Ning — where is he?"

"Loo Ning is dead," lied Ah. "We will celebrate; for now, by inheritance, you belong to me!"

Loo Kee looked at him gravely for a moment; then she jumped to her feet, laughing, and surveying him with admiration.

For Fah Now, in the gloom, the clock ticked drearily. In the sandal-wood frame on the wall the tiny flame flickered before the grimacing face of the joss. The two red tips of redolent tapers, stuck in a bowl of sand, smoldered forth small lazy smoke-lines of incense. Ah did not come; but there were sounds of revelry in the other room, and a lump pushed up in Fah Now's throat.

She could plainly hear the lady Kee tottering about on pigmy soles and laying dishes. She could tell when Kee ran to the closet, and, with an effort, mounted on a box to reach a top shelf. Placed there so that the child, Loo Wah, might not reach them, were the intricate Asiatic sweets and far-fetched titbits that were part circumstance on occasions of much candles and ceremony.   On it stood the big black jug of *moi-kwee-lo*, the amber rice-given gin which is flavored with roses and dosed with other things, and is known to hurry the generous heart.   Fah now was sure she heard the lady Kee draw the big jug along the shelf to lower it with mighty calculation, while Ah Koo took up Loo Ning's pipe — the one with the long, slim walking-stick stem and the bowl of an acorn's size. Why was the idle Loo Kee suddenly doing all this in the office of a tire-woman ?   Ah Koo had promised to make the small-foot woman bend before the lovely Fah Now, and braid Fah Now's glossy hair and anoint the former tire-woman's feet.   Was the mistress now being made to steep young tea-leaves and set out sugared water-melon rind and bean-meal cookies, so that Fah Now might sit behind Ah Koo at the table while Loo Kee stood to serve them ?   The sacrilege of such proceedings fought with the warm delight it stirred in her mind.   But it all fell through ; for why was she waiting alone, and in bonds, while Loo Kee had the company of the new master ?   Her little imagination could afford no clue, but the facts were constantly more plain to her from the sounds that came through the door.

When the bell in a distant tower spoke of two o'clock in the morning, the moon had long gone down, and the ringing came over silent house-tops through a sea-fog.   An hour had passed.   In the close room, dimmed by the ever-swaying flame before the joss, the stiffened captive was swallowing sobs.   Now what came from beyond the door had risen to the half-maudlin laughter of a revel reckoned in units of *moi-kwee-lo*.

There could be but little doubt of the perfidy of Ah Koo; but she would appear before them and see for herself if he, as master, meant to retain the old régime with Loo Kee, a proud and insolent mistress before whom Fah Now must quail. Fah Now dropped on her knees, and the chair followed her movement and fell with a rude shock against her shoulder. Her fingers were numb from the tying of the veins, and at least Ah Koo would release them when he saw her sufferings. She steadied herself painfully on her swollen wrists, and managed, inch by inch, to crawl toward where the light from the keyhole made a little sharp shaft in the darkness. The chair-top struck the door with a bump, and immediately the sounds on the other side stopped. She tried to rise; but the effort was too great, and she stumbled, and hit the door again. It burst open, and Fah Now tumbled flat on the floor with the chair on her back, and her face and garments woefully blackened by the dust. At this sudden apparition Ah Koo and Loo Kee broke into shouts of derisive laughter.

The two revelers sat at a table littered with scraps of food and wet with wasted liquor and tea. Kee's hair hung half unbraided at the hands of Ah, dragging the floor. Three tallow candles lit their faces, each flame casting a different shadow. A broken dish of syrup held the point of Loo Kee's elbow. The two laughed incontinently over the grotesque figure of Fah Now, who struggled to her feet, her face grown salmon-colored with mortification. Her head seemed ready to burst, and she moved back, yearning for the darkness, where they could not see her. But the chair stuck fast in the doorway, and she finally sank exhausted into it, with straining eyes.

"Pretty little cows!" shouted Ah to Kee, pointing at Fah Now's normal feet; and the two giggled at the sarcasm.

"What ghost is this?" asked Kee, nodding at the big foot woman.

"It is the heavenly joss come down from the wall!" cried the profane Ah. "Do reverence to it."

Loo Kee wheeled unsteadily to get the lamp which Loo Ning used to dry the opium bolus before he turned it into his pipe. The two knelt down before the strange figure of the scorned and fettered Fah Now, and took to simpering and jostling each other while they managed to light the lamp from the candles, spilling the oil and spotting themselves with grease. They set the oil cup on the floor just out of range of Fah Now's feet and placed the candles in a row and set a bowl of cookies in front of them. It was in imitation of a shrine and offering, with Fah Now representing the idol; and Ah Koo began a mock chant, while the nearly tipsy Kee held her sides in mirth. The two stood to survey their work in a lull that called again for the jug of *moi-kwee-lo*. Tears rolled down Fah Now's cheeks and she sought to dry them behind aching hands. But her hands were bound together.

At four o'clock Loo Kee had become drowsy, and Ah Koo left her stupidly lolling across the table. He cut the bonds from Fah Now's feet and silently let himself out of the rooms.

All Loo Kee remembered as she floated away on

the sleep of intoxication was that she had fastened a
golden butterfly pin on Ah Koo's cue. It was a
golden butterfly with green enameled wings — a gift
to her from Loo Ning. Ah Koo had forgotten that it
remained on his cue. In the open air the spirit of
moi-kwee-lo began to develop the effect he had thought
controllable. He was in a mood to smile and pride
himself over his conquest. There seemed nothing to
think of but the triumph over the man he had chosen
to make his enemy. The liquor was subliming, and
taking him through the air up over the hills toward
the laundry; — his feet did not seem to touch the
pavement. Ah Koo was beginning to lose his head.

Originally he had planned to come back to the
laundry in full possession of his faculties. The laundry, in a dark midnight, was a place suited to things
such as he had felt would surely happen. It stood
some way back from the street between two blind
walls. If he found Loo Ning weary with waiting on
the dilapidated veranda — watching over the big
square hole in it through which a man could jump on
the shoulders of an unsuspecting laundryman entering the basement where his fellows slept — then Ah
Koo had planned to punish Loo Ning. The laundrymen would find Loo Ning's body at six o'clock in the
morning, Ah Koo joining in their surprise. They
would hide the body in the basement to avoid inves-
tigation, and they would cleanse the steps with wash-
ing-lye.

Some one in the hours succeeding came and covered
the soundly sleeping lady Loo Kee as she lay on the
cold floor. Though she stirred not, hers was a trou-

bled sleep, always full of the image of the tortured
Fah Now, whose eyes stared at Kee, bulging in their
sockets and straining tears of blood.   In a little while
the midnight fog shroud rolled away and at length
the peep of dawn shot down from over Mount Diablo
on to the bay and the waking city.   In Chinatown,
where men rouse late in the morning of labor and live
in the night, this is the quietest hour.

The door where Fah Now had been held in durance
vile was closed and bolted.   The promise of day grew
dimly into the somber room through panes that were
soiled with seasons of dust and rain and through
hangings of young bamboos warped together with
skeins of worsted.   It rested first on the ebony table,
cold with half-burned candles and the broken dishes
of the night.   There came no sound, for Loo Kee
lay as one who had died in sleep.   When the light
had gained to cause gray shadows in her coverlet, and
when the black legs of chairs and stools stood barely
out against the walls, a something scraped across her
forehead.   The woman stirred a trifle and then as the
movement took place again, sluggishly raised her
hand to her brow.   The thing was the end of one of
the slim bamboos that made the window-hanging.   It
came again and again, like the swinging of a pendulum, and at last she opened her eyes, unaware of what
had aroused her.   The pendulum stopped.

Loo Kee stared vacantly at the ceiling, her cheeks
no longer red with rouge, but yellow pale from the
rubbing of her sleeve.   Then her eyes traveled down
the painted silken panels on the wall, gathering intel-
ligence as they went, to the scene of the late carouse.

They wandered over to the other side of the room and fixed.

In that unaccustomed corner some one was lying asleep, with his face turned to the wall. The form of his body rose roughly under the blankets, which were drawn up to his ears, half hiding his head. His cue appeared to be wound around his neck and under one ear, as if to make a softer berth. It was Loo Ning, thought Kee; but at the end of the cue she saw something glistening — the enameled butterfly. She remembered. Loo Ning was dead; she and all Loo Ning's possessions belonged to Ah Koo. And that was Ah Koo asleep in the corner — a man she rather liked. Ah then had made his departure a joke and had stolen back to put a pleasantry on her. She stifled a giggle — she would anticipate him.

The parting gloom discovered her face all smiling as she crawled stealthily along on hands and knees. When she felt she could just reach the tip of the cue, which lay invitingly, she stopped and held her breath in a pleasure of excitement. Then she gave the braid a tentative tug. Ah Koo turned a litt'e, but rolled unwillingly back, and she waited. Soon she pulled again, with something of a frown of impatience and with the same result. The light was not yet strong enough in the corner to show her whether he had waked and was feigning sleep to tease her; but she felt that it was so. She would cure him of that. Without a sound she rose on her elbow, brimming with the shout of merriment to come when he surrendered to the strain of his scalp. Then she braced herself and jerked the cue as hard as she could.

At that moment the bamboo hanging at the window behind her was quickly drawn aside and the light in the room was doubled. How it happened the woman did not know. Her mouth had opened wide, but stayed mute and gaping. The roots of her hair bristled and chilled, and her heart stopped. She fell forward in a swoon, with the tip of her finger touching the golden butterfly.

The robust Loo Ning, standing above, grim and middle-aged, surveyed her without emotion. He stepped over her, and without disturbing Ah Koo's head, removed from under the blankets two bundles of Loo Kee's apparel. The shape which had seemed to be that of Ah Koo's body collapsed into nothing.

Then he took up his pipe with the long slim walking-stick stem and the bowl of an acorn's size, and went out and spoke pleasantly to Fah Now.

THE POT OF FRIGHTFUL DOOM

HE blithesome air of "Tsim-tsam-chong" was issuing forth from the little chamber in Beverly Place when a sudden tempestuous rattling came at the door, and Dr. Wing Shee stilled his mandolin.

"They are going to finish my brother Chow!" wept the youth Sum Ah. "The head of the Sing Song Tong just gave me a scroll,—and a kick-push too,—and it says they have put Chow in chains in a dungeon, with nothing but foreign devils' bread! And the man who tries to rescue him they swear to roll in the cask-with-red-hot-spikes; and oh, most wonderful, ancient, wise physician, won't you try?"

Among the screens and china at Sum Chow's curio shop the doctor found none but the helper Yang. Chow was gone. Sum Fay, the diminutive wife of Sum Chow, heard, and put down her tiny girl Sum Oo, and came out with a sinking heart beneath her silken tunic. The doctor told her that Chow was his friend, and spoke of the duty Confucius demanded of friendship, and said that Sum Chow was surely beloved of the gods and so could not die young. Then he left her mute and blank. But he knew how fiercely the Sing Song Tong had scowled at Chow for years, because of Chow's buoyant career and because he would not join them. They were a treacherous secret society, driving women slaves, and seeking the despotism of Chinatown. A day ago their hatchet-men had eased a grudge against a poor old maker of pipe-bowl holes, and had clapped a plaster over his mouth, and beaten his back with his own bamboo, till his face was the color of clay, before Sum Chow had broken one of their heads and driven them away from their aged victim. Chow's present plight was the Sing Song Tong's reply; and now the doctor read the omen of three spots which he had shown Sum Chow the night before — spots which had been nine days on the doctor's thumb-nail. As the little old wise man pushed along the crowded streets, he strove to connect with all this the recent strange recurrence of the uninterpretable number one and a half, which had lately appeared in all his occult findings.

Sum Fay had gone with a shudder to the dusty shrine, and had lighted redolent joss-sticks, and burned soul-money for Chow's spiritual costs, in case they had killed him. She had been a mission Christian girl, and had learned but little of the Taoist faith; for all of Chow's religion was integrity and the love of family. But now, in her first disaster, her native promptings conquered; and she prayed to her tinseled gods with her baby in her arms. The tiny Sum Oo cooed and smilingly clutched at her mother's chin. But a salt tear suddenly dropped from Sum Fay's cheek into the baby girl's bright eye, and gave her a fright, and made her weep bitterly with her mother.

The doctor believed that if Sum Chow survived, he

was stalled in the Ok Hut private hospital, which
stood on a narrow street with evil history, called
Hatchet Run. The rascal Ok Hut was one of the
Sing Song Tong, and he had in his building a secret
cell which was entered through a trap in the garret
above the sick wards, and aired through a single
opening made by omitting a brick from the very deep
wall. To try an approach to this cell by way of Ok
Hut's garret would be futile, but Dr. Wing Shee knew
how to use the hole in the wall. When, at evening,
the learned doctor arrived at Hatchet Run, his sleeves
concealed many appropriate articles appertaining to
his plan. The doctor mounted to the room of his
great fat friend Pow Len, who dealt in tooth-picks
made from the whiskers of sea-lions, and whose heart
the doctor trusted more than his tongue.

"Ah!" said Pow Len. "It is he whose skill once
saved me from death of a twisted gullet. Can I serve
him?"

"It was not a twisted gullet," corrected the doctor,
assuming a heavy professional air. "Your complaint
was really contempt-of-the-spleen. My noble tooth-
pick friend, I wish to borrow your excellent coffin;
not for a funeral ceremony, but to sit in it here and
meditate. For my brain is heavy with invention."

"Nothing new, I hope?" said the orthodox Pow
Len, surveying the handsome casket which admiring
compatriots had given him. It stood as high as an
old-time eight-day clock.

"Consider a friend with confidence," quoted the
doctor. "My invention is classic, now remaining but
of fragmentary record, but first conceived ten centu-

7*

ries and three little years ago by the superhuman Tut Tut, to whom the thought shot down in a two-colored lightning stroke. It is the sky-flying machine."

"Ah!" exclaimed the vast Pow Len. "With that I could sail like a swallow to the Golden Gate, and beard the drowsy seals by night. Enormous profits — the life of a bird — dear me!"

"Precisely," said the doctor — "the life of the airy dodo. Now, in my experience, sir, nothing has proved so stimulating to precision of thought as sedentary solitude spent continuously in commodious coffins. Therefore I request your honorable death-chest."

Thus, after Pow Len, who listened with hanging lip, had reverently poured tea for the wonderful wise man, and, dreaming of innumerable toothpicks for the plucking, had agreed, under promise of secrecy, to exchange quarters with him until either the flying-machine was produced or suitable coffin rent forthcoming, Pow Len withdrew.

The doctor quickly locked the door, and then, with his wonted deftness, fitted the coffin-lid with hinges and a hook. In a little while he had screwed the box upright against the wall, and had blown out the light and fastened himself in what had been built for a silent man. The coffin was facing in the direction of the hospital. He emptied his sleeves, and hung a tiny peanut-oil lamp above his head, and by its glimmer began to drive an anger through the back of the coffin and through the unfinished sheathing of the house to the open air.

"Sum Chow would be such a loss," thought the doctor, as he worked in bare yellow arms, with his cue coiled around his neck, "that I cannot think the omens meant it. What pleasant hours we have passed learning the 'Melican tongue! Chow should have been a scholar; for the grace with which he handles, even in 'Melican script, such words as 'cat' and 'dok' and 'pik' and 'cow,' and a hundred others I forget, is marvelous. I do not think I could ever remember the complicated marks for 'man' and 'woo-man,' or 'poy' and 'kull' long enough to come from Sum Chow's and write them correctly in my room in Beverly Place, unless I sacrificed my dignity and ran. All this 'Melican writing looks alike."

An electric light high above a neighboring street shone on the hospital. Through the two auger-holes he could see the cell port left by the missing brick in the wall across the street. Now in one of the holes he fitted a bamboo tube, through which he intended to blow a message by way of the port to whomsoever should languish in the cell; and he hoped to reach Sum Chow. There were hours to pass before the street would be vacant, and Wing Shee had allotted the time to the composition of a message in verse, which to all but Chow would be gibberish. The doctor's only essay with a pen had left him content to express the English sounds as best he could with brush and Chinese characters. That was difficult when he met distinctions foreign to the older tongue; yet Chow could almost always decipher the doctor's scrolls. As when, in the beginning, Dr. Wing had written the Chinese signs for the sounds: "Wun pik kee foo lee too mut chee taw kee in hee sat: say iss no pik kee Chaw shee!" and Chow had readily translated these into "business" English as: "One piggee foolee too muchee talkee in his hat: say is no piggee jossee!" and recognized in this a phrase which had escaped from the mission night-school copy-book, and which, by disaster to the word "heart," had been changed from "The fool hath said in his heart" to "A big fool talked too much in his hat."

So the doctor made himself warm with the ardor of rhyming. Thus, while not many blocks away the little wife Sum Fay lay awake with the tiny Sum Oo asleep on her breast, and while the mother's melting eyes kept forming images of her husband in the dark, and she sighed and sobbed between hope and wretched fear, the doctor had even forgotten that he was sitting in a coffin, with the hour well past midnight, and the evidence of fiddle and pipe and maudlin festivity lessening in that neighborhood, and perhaps Sum Chow in extreme torture either in the hospital or in some place unknown. And when at length Sum Fay had fallen asleep with exhaustion, and the tiny Sum Oo heaved on the mother's breast like a voyager on a miniature sea, three long hours had passed, and the learned Dr. Wing Shee had finished the following English poem:

> How mun nee mah kee wah sun mai tum?
> How mun nee tay 'ko ah lee mah kee cum?
> You mak hop pee tem; yaw fah mee lee
> Ah too mut chee wai tai; no kun shee!
> You no me?

"And to think," sighed the doctor, "that, instead of staying by literature, I stampeded off to the wars! Instead of a leg-mender I might have been a laureate.

'Ah too mut chee wai tai; no kun shee!' Ah, Lao-Tse, but there's inspiration in this box!"

He softly unlocked the lid, and came out to scan the street through Pow's dilapidated blinds. For the moment there was no one in sight. Quickly he shut himself in again. A match was ready with its end embedded in putty so that the phosphorous was barely exposed. The putty fitted the bamboo tube, and when he sent this missile flying across the narrow street, propelled from the tube by an explosion of his breath, it disappeared within the hospital, through the port, without a sound. The flying-machine was completed.

SUM CHOW was in the hospital. He had been lured there by one to whom once he had given alms. The wretch had watched in the crowded thoroughfare for a man of distinguished dignity, wearing a rich blue tunic with bright gilt button-balls, and light blue silken trousers wrapped at the ankles. Sum Chow liked snowy linen stockings and shoes embroidered in silver; his long cue shone with careful braiding, and his head and face were always shaved close in Chinese elegance. He hardly betrayed the power of attack which had made his envied success. That day he had gone to Hatchet Run to pay for a golden love-bangle for littlest Oo. The appointed traitor had begged a hearing in the hospital entry, and there six brutal Sing Song hatchet-men had soon prevailed over Chow's single strength. He had battered two of them, but the others had thrust him into a big jute bag, and when they carried him wriggling through the wards and up the garret ladder, the patients thought it merely a crazy opium-fiend. The hatchet-men had emptied the bag through the trap to the brick floor, and Chow had been stunned, and had wakened to find himself cold and stiff in semi-darkness, at first he knew not where. He had put his mouth to the hole in the wall and called for help in all the languages he knew, but no one had heard him. He had lain aching for hours afterward, during which Ok Hut's menial had lowered a bowl of water and some American bread. These he had avoided with fear; and so hunger sharpened, and he sternly set his face to the fate which he felt was preparing. He wondered if his shade could protect his little wife and his littlest Oo, or if death was even harsh in that. Midnight found him cramped and bowed. The strange thing which suddenly struck the inner wall, and fell a-flame at his side, was startling even to Chow.

It smoldered and died. In a moment another missile, with more wood exposed to the flame, struck and ignited. He seized it, and it burned brightly long enough for him to notice that immediately following it a waxen taper, tipped with its balancing putty ball, had shot through the air port, long, white, and unmistakable. He lighted it, and the cell port appeared from without to be faintly illumined. When his eyes had changed to meet the light, the wondering Chow picked up a scroll, and instantly recognized the brushwork of the doctor. He read:

> How many markee was on my thumb?
> How many days 'go allee markee come?
> You make happy time; your family
> Are too muchee wet-eyed: no can see!
> You know me?

He bounded into life, and waved the taper past the
port three times for the spots the doctor had shown
him the night before, and then, after a pause, nine
times for the days they had stayed on the thumb nail.
So that Chow, drawing on a thread that flew in attached to a pebble, was not surprised to find one end
of a Chinese telephone, and then to hear the voice of
his friend :

"Worship the gods for this preservation, hearty
brother," it whispered. "Your little Fay and little Oo
and the stripling all fare well, though wet-eyed that
you stay away; and be felicitated on their mighty love.
Now first I will shoot you a dinner of dried ducks'
hearts in tiny gelatin capsules — those capsules which
the 'Melicans use to hide the taste of their grimacing
drug *kwain-nai-in*, but which were long conceived before the year of their principal joss by one Muk Ah
Muk, who confined in them the bubblesome spirits he
extracted from his ten meek wives."

So that as he fell asleep, bodily contented and hopeful for the morrow, Sum Chow murmured for the
tenth time :

"With the gods I never associated; but of mortals
surely the greatest is Dr. Wing Shee !"

THE letter which reached the saddened curio shop
told in the doctor's Chinese-written English that the
big yellow tea-pot was not smashed, but endured in
eternal tenderness for its little cup and its littlest
saucer and the young spoon. Sum Ah (the young
spoon) translated this for joyous Sum Fay (the little
cup), and she danced Sum Oo (the littlest saucer) on
her knee, who laughed and gurgled and behaved not

like a demure Cantonese, but like any sprite amused
by its own half helplessness. The light seemed now
to warm the strange and beautiful wares to brighter
tones, and Sum Fay set gaily to dust them before a
customer from the foreign devils' world should send
her scuttling in her slippers back to the penetralia;
and when the helper Yang took up his books in an
easier mood, and rattled the buttons on the abacus,
Sum Ah sang a mission hymn of hallelujah. The
better feeling lasted well into the day; but though
in the afternoon Sum Fay walked abroad behind Sum
Ah, and bravely smiled and chatted with him that
none might suspect her woe, twilight fell with deeper
melancholy. Dr. Wing had given no hope for the
future. If the beloved had been free, he would have
run to find his wife and his funny baby.

In the small hours of another weary night Sum
Chow sat on the damp cell floor despairing again. In
the morning Ok Hut had come to the trap and
beamed down, wearing the rings the hatchet-men had
wrested from Chow. Ok Hut had observed with an
affectation of scientific glee the signs of the first day's
suffering and then had departed. The hours had
dragged without incident, and darkness had come,
and then midnight, with ominous sounds from the
pauper ward, and two o'clock, with its anxious expectancy; and then the appointed time had passed with
no token from Dr. Wing. The picture kept growing
in Chow's mind of the doctor, dead and cold in Pow
Len's coffin at the hands of the Sing Song Tong, and
then of a cortège, with little Fay mourning the friend

of her widowhood.   By now he had hoped to be free.
The plan had been to cut a hole in the trap, which
would serve when he jumped and reached through to
slide the bolt.   But the sawing of wood in the stillness of night must be slow and exceedingly careful;
and now it was late for beginning, and he had yet no
tools.

Across the way the learned doctor, with the peanut-
oil lamp like an aureole above his head, was standing
motionless in the dim mahogany casket, frowning at
sounds from the hospital.   The doctor's trusted omens,
whether he consulted the spots on his neighbor's cloth,
or the bundle of crooked sticks in the pewter mug, or
which way a bug ran under the burning-glass, had
haunted him still with the uncanny number one and
a half.   He waited, alert for good or evil containing
that element.   The moans in the pauper ward were
holding him back.   They rose from a wretch in the
sinking stage of the opium-habit, one of those whom
the sick-pay tongs sent thither to save the drain on
their treasuries.   Ok Hut was accustomed to give
these victims a draught which promised relief to their
agonies, and then, in the most exquisite dream of their
lives, they floated out of the world with never a murmur at fate, and the societies gained, and Ok Hut
prospered, and the coroner was amused.   Sometimes
were heard for a moment those screams that went
with the final plight of the smoke fiends, when, as
frequently happened, they suddenly lost their minds
and ran amuck; but then Ok Hut, if they refused the
fatal dose, would shut them in the secret cell, stuffing
the air port with rags.   The doctor feared that such

might happen to-night in the midst of Chow's endeavor.

But the groans subsided, and the lights from the hospital windows lessened, and Hatchet Run was left in silence. Sum Chow heaved a mighty sigh as the telephone pebble flew in; and now he pulled on the endless rope-yarn rigged across the street by the doctor, and brought in the tools through the air-port. Also the doctor sent a small round object in many thicknesses of wadding.

"Handle it like a new-born babe," he had whispered; "for in it are crowded winds of whirling waterspouts, and thunder of falling mountains, and flashes of furious flame. 'T is a pot of frightful doom, tuned to the omens with one and a half frog's thumbs."

Then Sum Chow poised on the empty water-bowl, and started the auger into the trap. But suddenly he paused.

There had come a wild shriek from the pauper ward, with commotion and the smashing of a chair and the calls of the terrified sick. Ok Hut had been deceived. The opium fiend had not been done for; he had risen up and fallen on Ok Hut in his sleep, throttling him, and screaming that the room was hot with fiery demons.

"Ah!" muttered the doctor, in alarm. "The noise will scurry them all from their beds. Ah!"

Sum Chow withdrew the auger, and listened. They were dragging the madman up the ladder; they were going to throw him also into the cell. The ladder broke, and three men fell to the floor with a crash. That meant a delay, thought Chow. He sunk the auger into a beam close by the trap, and worked until it was twisted firmly several inches into the wood. Now it was stout enough to hold him when he hung to it by one arm — near enough to the trap to clutch the ankle of whomsoever should come to open it.

Ok Hut's menial, a man from the northern province of Chang Tung, great in stature, but no match in quickness for a well-built Cantonese, was treading along the garret. Sum Chow sprang up and clung to the auger, and the door was raised in the dark.

"You are free," came the menial's voice, speaking falsely, as Chow well knew. "I will tie this cord, and you can climb up on it."

This was a ruse. Ok Hut feared that the squad might have heard the cries, and might be closing in from the outside, suspicious of something irregular. They had done this once before, and then they had found simply a wretch beating out his brains against the hospital floor. But to-night they might have been warned and might be looking for Chow, though an appeal to the police on behalf of any Chinaman is improbable; and they might, when all expectation should subside, swoop suddenly down as they had before. It was better to get Chow out and lock him in a chest in the garret, though at the risk of stifling him. Then the madman could be thrown into the cell, where if the squad came before his strength had been writhed away they would find at the worst but a poor victim whose condition, brought on by himself, would not excite the anger of the law. The menial's invitation to Chow was a ruse which meant that when Chow's head was within reach a noose would be slipped over it, choking him, so that he would mutely follow the menial, for whatever temporary disposition might be made of him during the time.

The menial waited for an answer, but the place was black and silent. He spoke again, but his voice was returned by the walls of the cell. Then he went on his knees and struck a match, and thrust it down to be away from its sulphurous fumes. The match sputtered its first blue flame, and at the same moment the menial's wrist was caught by two hands, and the full weight of Sum Chow came on the menial's arm with such sudden force that he fell forward, hitting his head on the trap-way, and then tumbled through to the floor of the cell, where he lay stunned.

In the house on the other side of the street the doctor was breathlessly on tiptoe, with the telephone at his ear. The telephone line hung lax, and the hospital was grimly still.

"Go into the street, O bravest friend!" at length came a trembling voice in the doctor's ear. "Haul and hold fast on the cord. It hangs out from the hole in the wall. That one of us who lives shall avenge my little Fay, O friend! my littlest Oo! Haul and hold fast!"

"I hear," came the quiet answer. "Friends to live with — enemies to die with. Haul and hold fast!"

The doctor let himself noiselessly out of the coffin. It was dangerous to descend by the stairs. In a moment he dropped from the window, three times his length, to the pavement. At first he lay as if disabled, but he soon staggered up, and found the cord that issued from the cell port. The other end Sum Chow

had tied around the menial's head and through his
mouth to keep him silent, and Chow had made the man
rise and had forced him against the cell port, where
the doctor, now hauling and holding fast on the cord
from the street below, held him powerless to move or
speak.   A long time seemed to pass while the doctor
leaned back with the cord wrapped around his wrist.
To him the hospital appeared to have regained its
slumbers, and he pictured Sum Chow creeping stealthily along the garret toward the ladder-way.   On
the Run the swaying shop-signs squeaked in the
gusty wind that was bringing the dawn.   The doctor
heard the steps of one of the squad on the intersect-
ing street, and described the arc of a circle that
brought him around the corner, still taut on the
cord, but safe from observation.   The policeman went
by, and one approached from another way, and the
doctor swung back into Hatchet Run.

Sum Chow had climbed out of the cell.   At a distance he saw the faint light from the ladder-way, but
heard nothing.   In a few moments he walked toward
it, knowing that the tread would be taken for that of
the menial.   At the ladder he peered cautiously over.
The room was one apart from the sick wards, and no
one was in it.   The maniac seemed to have been
quieted, and doubtless lay in his bunk.   The prisoner
hung by one hand, and dropped to the floor of the
hospital; at the same instant Ok Hut appeared at the
door from the pauper ward, and stopped, transfixed
with astonishment.   For a moment the two men stood
staring into each other's eyes.

"This is life or death to you," said Chow, in a low

8

tone. "Throw up your hands and turn your face to the wall."

But Ok Hut did not obey. He kept his eyes on Chow, debating. Ok had no weapon, but there was one in the drawer of the table where the feeble lamp stood burning. Sum Chow also seemed unarmed, except for a small object which he grasped. Ok Hut waited, planning how to shorten the space between himself and the table, so as to make a dash and get it sooner than Chow could reach him. There was silence but for the snoring of those who slept in the pauper ward. Ok Hut seemed motionless; but he was changing his weight from one foot to another, so that each time he was approaching a fraction of an inch nearer the weapon that lay in the drawer.

Over in the other building some one was looking in perplexity from the window at the spectacle of the learned Dr. Wing Shee holding tight on a cord from the cell port. It might be friend or foe. The doctor jammed his slouch hat over his eyes, and felt for the revolver that was strapped to his forearm under his large sleeve. Soon the enemy would be down and out and at him, and there would be pistol shots and the hurry of the squad in the night.

In the hospital the two men were gazing intensely into each other's eyes. Ok Hut was beginning to move by greater units, and his confidence began to return.

"Stop!" said Chow, putting out his hand. "If you pass that crack in the board —"

But Ok Hut made a leap for the table. In a twinkling Chow, with all his might, hurled the pot of doom.

A terrific explosion in Chinatown startled the hills of San Francisco, followed by cries, the jingle of window-glass, and the chattering of scared Chinese, and soon by comparative stillness. Sum Chow, with a flesh-wound in his cheek, came bounding down from the hospital into the arms of the doctor. Mingled cries were rising from the sick wards. The Run was filling with a crowd of all races that seemingly had sprung from nowhere.

Already smoke was pouring from the hospital windows.

"Conceal your cut," commanded the doctor. "Stand as though you were one of the crowd. In a moment the squad will be here, and then the ruthless water-snake men, with their chu-chu monster."

When the police thrust them aside, the two crossed to the door of a friendly merchant, and soon were hidden in the collecting throng. They stayed to see Ok Hut brought out insensible and bleeding from many wounds, and all the other inmates brought out safely. When Chow and the doctor knew that the building was doomed, they issued unmolested from the back of the store to another street, and made their way in the early light toward where little Fay lay awake, with her heart beating fast at the shouts and the clang of the fire-engines, with littlest slumbering Oo clasped tight to her bosom.

THAT evening they sat about the dinner-table, with Sum Ah and the helper Yang, who listened in admiration, while happy little Fay sat behind her spouse, and littlest Oo enchanted herself with the tip of the doctor's cue.

"You — you risked your life for me!" said Chow, with something glistening in his eye.

"And what is amusing," said the learned Dr. Wing Shoe, who would have risked it again, "is that they have amputated one of Ok Hut's legs at the knee. So that the omen 'one and a half' meant simply that he was doomed to issue from this with only one and a half of his two original legs! I have to thank you for these very interesting and exciting days."

CHAN TOW, THE HIGHROB

8*

EFORE me sits the Chinese — my friend who, when the hurly-burly 's done, spins me out the hours with narratives of ancient Yellow-land. His name is Fuey Fong, and he speaks to me thus:

"Missa Gordon, whatta is Chrisinjin Indevil Shoshiety?"

I explain to him as best I can the purpose of the Society for Christian Endeavor.

"We', dissa morning I go down to lailload station. Shee vay many peoples getta on tlain. Assa conductor, 'Whatta is?' Conductor tole me: 'You can't go. You a *heeffen*. Dissa *Chrisinjin* Indevil Shoshiety.'

"Dissa mek me vay tire'. 'Me'ican peoples fink ole China heeffen. Fink doan' know about Gaw of heffen. Dissa 'Me'icans doan' know whatta is. China peoples benieve Olemighty Gaw semma lika you."

Fuey endures in meditation several moments. Then he says:

"Missa Gordon, I tay you how about Gaw convert China clilimal?"

"How God converted a Chinese criminal?"

"Yeh. I tay you. Dissa case somma lika dis:

119

"One tem was China highrob. His nem was Chan Tow. Live by rob on pubnic highway evely one he can. Dissa highrob live in place call Kan Suh. We', one tem was merchan', nem Jan Han Sun, getta lich in Kan Suh; say hisse'f: 'I getta lich; now mus' go home Tsan Ran Foo, shee my de-ah fadder-mudder-in-'aw an' my de-ah wife.' So med determine to go home nex' day.

"Kan Suh to Tsan Ran Foo about dousands miles distant, and dissa parts China no lailload, no canal. So dissa trivveler declude to ride in horse-carry-chair."

"What is a horse-carry-chair?"

"We', I tay you. Somma like dis: Two horse — one befront, one inhine. Two long stick, and carry-chair in minnle. Usa roop somma lika harness. Dissa way trivvle long distance ole ove' China.

"We', nex' day Missa Jan start out faw Tsan Ran Foo in horse-carry-chair. Hed big backage of go' an' sivver. By-by — trivvle long tem — was pass high tree. Up high tree was Chan Tow — dissa highrob — was very bad man! Chan Tow up tree to watch to stea' whatta he can, semma lika vutture."

"Like a *vutture*?"

"Like a vutture — big bird — eat dead beas' ole he can.

"Chan Tow look down on load, and shee horse-carry-chair wif Missa Jan feet stick out. Nen dissa highrob say hisse'f: 'Vay nice feet; lich man. I go fonnow him. Maybe can stea' from him.' So fonnow 'long Missa Jan by day, by night, severow day — doan' lose sight ole dissa tem. By-by Missa Jan was trivvle ole night, and leach hotel early morning. He tole

hotel-kipper: 'You giva me loom. I slip ole day.'
Nen tek his backage go' an' sivver, an' tek to bed wif
him. Chan Tow come long, say: 'Giva me loom
nex' my de-ah frien' jussa come in horse-carry-chair.'
Hotel-kipper look him, and say, 'Whatta your nem
is?' Chan Tow say, 'My nem Chow Ying Hoo.'
Dissa nem, transnate Ingernish, mean Brev Tiger."

"And what does Chan Tow mean?"

"Oh, Chan Tow mean ole semma bad faminy.

"We', dissa highrob slip nex' loom Missa Jan; but
no can fine how to rob him ole dissa tem. Getta vay
much disgussion; but nex' day he fonnow long inhine
dissa lich man jussa semma befaw. Somma tem eat
at semma tabuh wif Jan; but Jan getta begin to suspicious, an' ole tem getta his go' an' sivver unnerneaf
him when he shet down to tabuh. Chan Tow say hisse'f: 'You fink I doan' know how to shueshess to
stea' yo' money. Maybe I big foo' you.'

"We', by-by was mont' go by. Dissa merchan'
reach his netive sheety. Firs' he go immedinity to
respec' his fadder-mudder-in-'aw, becose his fadder-
mudder dead. Dey vay gnad to shee him — vay denight. Dey assa him vay many quishuns; but he tole
dem: 'I mus' go to my de-ah wife. I not sheen her
so long tem.' Nen he smi' hisse'f, an' tole horse-carry-
chair-man run wif him quick to fine his de-ah wife.
When he allive ne' his house, say to man: "Goo'-by!
I go ressa way on feetsteps.' Nen go vay quier on his
tiptoe, and lock vay soft at his daw."

Here pauses the Chinese, and looks at me. Shortly
he says:

"We'?"

"Well?" I echo.

"We', dissa last tem dissa merchan' Jan Han Sun was sheen annibe!"

"Does the highrob follow him and kill him?"

"No one shee any highrob. No one see any horse-carry-chair-man. No one shee any Jan. No maw!

"Nex' morning come fadder-mudder-in-'aw to con-gratchnate dissa daughter. Said, 'We vay denight, vay gnad, yo' husban' come home. Where he is dissa morning? Daughter look vay supp'ise'. Said, 'When you shee my husban' come home?' Parents said: 'Why, my de-ah daughter, yo' husban' pass by my daw las' night. We hev vay short convisition beged-der, an' he say bling home glate many go' an' sivver — mek you habby. Nen left us come shee you.'

"Nen, vay suddenity, dissa daughter say: 'I fink you ki' my husban', so you can rob! I hev you arres'.'

"An' she go to magistrate an' mek petition. Say her fadder-mudder to ki' her husban'. Her fadder-mudder bofe vay indignant; but was putta in jai'.

"Magistrate examine case, assa many quishuns, search bofe dissa house — but can't fine who mudder dissa merchan'. Fadder-mudder-in-'aw say, 'We in-nocent.' Daughter say, 'You liars!' Her parents med declaration, 'I doan' hed mudder to any person.' Two mont's go by. Can't find who mudder. Nen daughter petition to supere court; say dissa magis-trate doan' know how fine who mudder. Supere court send word, 'You doan' fine who mudder in six mont's — deglade yo' lank.' Dissa China way to mek law.

"We', dissa magistrate, whatta he do? Doan' like

getta deglade; dissa spoi' his whole life. Say hisse'f:
' I vay detest to get deglade. Mus' go mek detectif —
fine who mudder.' Nex' day left his court, and go
mek long trivvle — ole dress up like a fortune-tayer."

" Like a fortune-teller ? "

" Yeh; fortune-tayer. Vay low common in China.
Go roun' wif ole kine bad peoples.

" Magistrate look jussa semma somma poh fortune-
tayer. Nen go out on load an' trivvle — trivvle vay
far. Eve'y tem shee a man look lika somma bad man,
try mek frien's wif him. But no can fine who mudder.
Long tem trivvle — 'way intchuh China; but no can
fine any one knows about dissa case. Say hisse'f:
' Pitty soon I getta much discoulagement. Two
mont's maw, getta deglade, getta disglace! I doan'
know I ki' hisse'f ! '

" One day was stag' 'long load; getta mos' exhaus'.
Bofe sides load was high heels, no house. Kep' on,
on; semma heels; semma no house; mus' lie down
in load wifout any subber, wifout any dlink. Dissa
magistrate begin getta desplate. Nen he fink, 'I play
to Gaw an' my ancestors.' So begin play lika diss:
'O Gaw, O my ancestors, givva me res'; givva me
foo'; givva me wadder! Nen I kip on fawever fine
who ki' Jan Han Sun.' Nen magistrate stag' 'long
few steps, an' dlop down on big lock. No *can* any
fudder.

" Pitty soon look roun'; shee litty light shine from
winnidow. Dissa was littyoshantyhouse — vay poh
look — "

" Littyoshantyhouse ? "

" Litty — ole — shanty — house!

"We', magistrate go lock at daw. Come to daw littyoneddy — "

"Little old what?"

"Litty — ole — neddy!"

"Dissa oneddy she was vay ole, vay febble. He tole her: 'Please, oneddy, you givva me kunderness let me go slip in yo' house to-night! I 'mos' died. No subber, no wadder — mos' exhaus'!' Oneddy tole him: 'Walks in; walks in! But you mus' kip vay quier, my de-ah sir; as quier as can be! My son is dreffel differcut man. His profussion was highrob. He getta home minnernight; an' you doan' kip quier, I fred he to strike you!' But magistrate say: 'I too tire to getta scare'. You nedda me stay wif you.'

"So oneddy giva him to eat, an' show him to go slip unner tabuh in katchen. Nen he lie down, an' play once more his ancestors an' Gaw: 'You he'p me oleleddy; I kip plomise. You he'p me somma maw — I fine who mudder.' Nen go slip.

"By-by was dleam 'bout gleen moudens, gleen wadder. Hear' spi'its say, 'I wi' assist you.' Ole dissa vay good sign. Suddinity was wek up from his slip, and shaw oneddy stand befaw him — ole in dark. She say: 'My son come home in vay good humors. Say lika mek yo' acquaintance.' Dissa tem was minnernight. Magistrate craw' out from unner tabuh, an' fonnow oneddy in nex' loom. Heah was Chan Tow, dissa highrob. Was fee' in vay good tempiniment to-night — hedda jus' rob litty gir' her earlings."

"It made him very happy to have stolen earrings from a little girl?"

"Oh, yeh. Earlings med jay-stone.

"We', Chan Tow he vay denight to shee dissa fortune-tayer. Mek put hisse'f down to tabuh, eat subbah wif him, an' mek oneddy hop 'long getta ole bes' was in oshantyhouse. Chan Tow say: 'My de-ah sir, I am exceediny denight to shee you. We bofe about sem professions: you fortune-tayer; I was highrob.' Nen bofe eat, dlink long tem, an' Chan Tow tay ole about his shueshess in binniziz."

"You mean business?"

"Yeh; binniziz.

"Tay ole about his binniziz. Tay how stea' watch from 'Me'ican missiolary man. Tay how—"

"How did he steal the watch from the American missionary?"

"We', somma lika dis: Chan Tow was vay stlong man, but vay litty meat on his boles. One day shee missiolary man come 'long load. Hedda watch-chain hang out. Chan Tow lie down in load, an' begin kick an' scleam ole semma sick white woman. Missiolary man was vay sympafy, an' tole him, 'Whatta is?' Chan Tow say: 'Mucha vay sick! Much vay sick! You no he'p me home I getta died! You tekka me home I mek good Chrisinjin boy!' Missiolary man vay good man; say hisse'f: 'Gaw sen' me dissa man mek convict to Chrisinjanity. I he'p him!' So tek up Chan Tow in his arm to tek home. Chan Tow kep' gloan, gloan,—an' ole dissa tem was put his han' in missiolary his pocket an' stea' dissa watch! Nen Chan Tow kep' hang on missiolary his neck an' say hisse'f: 'I lika dissa to ride better I lika to walk. I letta dissa missiolary man ca'y me jusso far he can.' So missiolary man stag' 'long tem 'long load, an' kep'

sweat, sweat — semma lika glass ice-wadder; an' Chan
Tow kep' gloan semma like ole barn daw."

"Chan Tow kept groaning like an old barn door,
and the missionary man kept perspiring like a glass
of ice-water?"

"Oh, no! Missiolary man sweat. By-by, hedda
ca'y dissa highrob two miles — 'way down vanney,
'way up heel. Nen missiolary man lose ole his breffs,
an' begin to gaps. He say, 'Mus' res'; mus' putta
you down!' Chan Tow kep' gloan, an' say: 'You
putta me down I doan' know I die. Mus' getta home!'
Missiolary man say: 'Can't he'p — I 'mos' exhaus'.'
Nen dissa highrob jump down vay well, an' say:
'We', I mus' getta home. I walk ressa way — leave
you to res'. Goo'-by!' Nen run fas' he can down
dissa heel.

"Missiolary man stay look him run, an' kep' fink
ole tem. Nen say hisse'f: 'I fink dissa man inshin-
sherity. I lose ole dissa tem wif him! Whatta tem
it is?' Nen he search his watch. 'Oh, my! No
watch; no convict! Dissa vay bad day!'"

The Chinese grins with the greatest pleasure.

"We', magistrate an' highrob kep' tay ole 'bout ex-
pelunces in binniziz."

"*Business!*"

"Yep; *binniziz.*"

"Kep' tay ole about binniziz. By-by pea-oil light
go out. Oneddy craw' up on bed an' go slip. Nen
two men stay an' smoke pipe — ole dark. Magistrate
closs his legs an' say, ole lika he doan' care: 'Missa
Highrob, dissa light go out mek me remin' whatta
habben Tsan Ran Foo. You heard about dissa case?

Man nem Jan Han Sun go home his wife — no can
fine who mudda.' Chan Tow smi' vay plou', an' say:
'Oh, my de-ah brudder, I know ole 'bout dissa case.
I was to shee dissa man getta ki' in his own houses.'

"Magistrate dlaw glate big breff frough his pipe.
Swallow smoke clea' down his stomach! Mek big
cough — nearny cough his top head off! — an' wek
oneddy! Nen he say: 'We', we'! You good dea'
maw wise dissa Magistrate Tsan Ran Foo. I hea' he
was deglade his rank. Cannot fine who mudder!'

"Chan Tow say: 'Dissa magistrate mus' come fine
me. No one ess can tay him. I tay you ole about
dissa mudder. You lika hea'?' Magistrate say: 'We',
I vay tire'. But lika hea' you talk better I lika go
slip, my de-ah sir!' Dissa mek highrob vay plou', an'
he begin lika dis:

"'One day shaw horse-carry-chair trivvle 'long load.
Shaw feet stick out — vay nice feet; mus' be lich man.
So fonnow him. He hev big backage go' an' sivver,
but eve'y tem go subbah mus' oleways shet hisse'f on
top dissa backage. Fonnow him long tem — severow
weeks. But cannot stea' from him. By-by he
reach his home Tsan Ran Foo, an' go to respec' his
mudder-fadder-in-'aw; nen go fine his wife. Dissa
tem was minnernight — vay dark. Fink was good
tem to stea' from him, an' getta his go' an' sivver. So
kep' fonnow 'long load. When he getta his house he
lock long tem at his daw, but was no answer. Nen
say, vay loud: "De-ah wife, letta me in! I am yo'
de-ah husban' come home." So by-by was daw open,
an' his wife come say: "Oh my de-ah husban'! so
denight to shee you!" Nen ole dark.

"'Nen I go roun' back his house. Getta 'long bamboo po', an' putta dissa po' up 'gainst house to shin up dissa loof. Nen cut with knife litty roun' ho' frough loof, an' look down into dissa house. Can look down into loom, an' shee ole whatta was habben.

"'Vay soon Jan examine tabuh; say: "O my de-ah wife, whatta for you setta dissa tabuh for two peoples? You have comply?" Wife say: "O my de-ah husban', eve'y tem since you go 'way I setta dissa tabuh for two peoples—you and me—jussa semma you heah!" Jan smi' vay plou', an' say, "You are shinsherny my de-ah wife!"—was mak fee' vay good.

"'Nen his wife tole him: "Now we hev jubinee; eat, dlink—mek me'y tem!" So I lie on top dissa loof, vay dly, vay hunger; an' ole tem shee her husban' eat subbah an' kip dlink, dlink, an' kiss his wife, an' dlink, an' getta maw an' maw intosheate. Byby was so intosheate mus' go slip. Nen his wife he'p him go bed, an' he begin snow."

"How 's that?"

"Begin snow — snowul — snole! Begin snole!"

"It began to snow?"

"Oh, no; I tay you. Dissa merchan' begin mekka lika dis." Fuey makes a sound that is unmistakable.

"'We', nen look shee whatta dissa woman go do. She go to hooks on wa', an' tek down lot her dresses. Nen I shee man step out. Dissa woman whisper to him: "Shee my husban' slip. He bling back glate many go' and sivver! You love me, you tekka dissa sharp knife and ki' him. Nen we getta marry begedder to-morrow, an' mek habby tem."

"'Her beau say: "Oh, no. I fred ki' him. Fred I

get behead." An' nen dissa woman getta vay mad wif him, an' say: "You doan' ki' him, I tekka dissa knife an' chot op yo' head op, instamentty!" Nen he begin tek off his mine —'"

"Took off his mind?"

"Yeh," says Fuey; "I don't know dissa word — semma you tek off yo' clo's."

"Changed his mind?"

"Yeh."

"'Begin to tek off — chenge his mine — an say: "How I ki' him?" Woman say: "You tekka dissa sharp knife."

"'Nen he clep' up to dissa bed, his eye ole stick out from his head. When he getta where dissa merchan' slip, an' snow, snow, ole semma hev good dleam, dissa beau mek lika was to chenge his mine 'gain; but dissa woman whisper: "Quick! Quick!"— an' nen ole sudden dissa beau stlike. Nen Jan Han Sun was died — instamentty!

"'Dissa woman begin to rip up flaw. Her beau he'p her ole he can, an' work vay hard, fas'— fred somebody come. Kep' look 'roun'. An' eve'y tem pea-oil light flicker, look round to shee who was. Ole tem stop to hol' his ear on flaw — shee who come. Flaw rip up; nen go getta shover an' dig big long ho' in earf, unnerneaf dissa bed. Nen putta dissa merchan' his body in dissa ho' in groun'. Nen vay quick shover back ole dissa earf, fix flaw, an' blow out light.

"'Ole tem I stay up dissa loof. Vay hunger — no wadder; an' cannot rob dissa merchan' becose he dead! Getta vay disgussion. Light go out, I hang foot ove' side dissa loof, an' begin fink. Maw I fink,

9

maw getta disgussion. By-by getta *vay, vay* disgussion. Nen tek dissa bamboo po' to shove frough
dissa ho' in loof — vay quier. When he shove frough,
nen I ole suddenity begin push, jab, shove — quick —
ole semma churn budder. Down below woman an'
her beau begin squea', squea', ole semma rat! 'Mos
scare' to def! Nen I shin down loof — run 'way.' "

Fuey draws a long breath, and smiles at me his
calm, celestial smile.

"We', Chan Tow finis' his sto'y. Magistrate was
ole tem smoke big clou's smoke, an' mek loom look
lika was on fire. Mek oneddy wek up an' open daw.
When Chan Tow finis', magistrate say: 'My de-ah
brudder de highrob, yo' sto'y vay intinesse, vay intinesse! I fink I go slip.' So ole thlee was lie down
to go slip, an' Chan Tow was tek his opi' pipe an' begin smoke opi.' Whatta you say — hurt the pipe?'"

"Hit the pipe."

"Oh, yeh; hit pipe. I doan' spe'k Ingernish vay
we'.

"Magistrate wet long tem. By-by oneddy begin
to snow, an' nen by-by Chan Tow getta doan'
know."

"Chan Tow got *don't know ?* "

"Getta all semma was died. Doan' know."

"Unconscious?"

"Yeh; uh-uh-coshious!" sneezes Fuey.

"Nen magistrate begin craw' 'long on his stomach
— inchy — inchy — cross flaw out daw. Nen run fas'
he can toward Tsan Ran Foo.

"One mont' go by, an' magistrate sit up in his high
chair in his court. Befront him dissa woman an' her

beau,— ole cover wif mark dissa bamboo po',— an'
dissa fadder-mudder-in-'aw, an' dissa highrob.   Magistrate say vay slow — ole semma idol talk: '*Dissa —
woman — her lover — are convert — to behead — by her
dey heads cut off — till dey dead!*   What you fink,
woman?' Woman say: 'Yo' Excennency, I vay gnad
to be behead wif my de-ah lover.   I vay satisfaction
we behead begedder.   Our spi'its begedder happy
fo'ever.' Nen she turn kiss her beau; but he too
scare to spe'k. An' bof was tek out to behead — dissa
woman ole tem to mek to kiss her beau.

"Magistrate say to highrob: 'You know me?
Who eata subba wif you sucha-sucha night?' Chan
Tow say, 'O yo' Excennency, I doan' know who was!'
Magistrate say: 'I was dissa man. I glate t'anks faw
you. Awso dissa fadder-mudder-in-'aw dissa dead
man. Gaw sen' me to yo' house to mek you instlu-
ment to convert dissa mudderers. I give you good
position; awso money.'"

"And that was how these criminals were *converted?*" I say, remembering the promise of the
story.

"Yeh; convert to behead. Dissa case," concluded
Fuey, "show how Gaw can convert climinal when he
wish; show how Gaw is glate. I tay you China peoples not heeffen. China 'ligion teach to try to affection one anudder; respec' yo' parents; an' charity an'
pure moral. If people do right I fink he shall be
saved."

A LITTLE LIBERAL

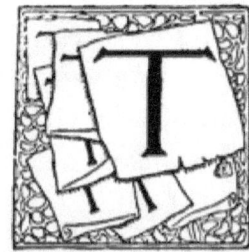HE train whisked off in a dust, and, for the first time in his life, the son of Alexander the Liberal and of Violet the Modern had parted from them. They were his playmates; and a passage of clouds across the sun would have swung the balance to tears. But it was Maine, and a blithesome July day, and Uncle Jasper Bennett was light-hearted when he forgot his Maker. They rattled off behind the angular mare Polly between stone-walls and stony fields and under hemlock-trees. How soon? asked the Boy. Were there any little pigs — any little bits of ones? Was there yet a spinning-wheel — a real one, and not like those that were only made? And, last and most, O, were there still some fishes in that dark, deep pool, down beneath the willows?

At length loomed the homestead, in a setting of mighty elms; low sheds, and a vast red barn with the swallows in and out, and a stark white dwelling-house with sleeping blinds. In the orchard a score of gravestones — a ghostly garden of Bennetts since the century came in; and, standing on the porch by the kitchen door, Aunt Hepzibah.

She was comely, though they said her eyes were

cold, like the clouded sea; and she was wonderfully well
preserved. She had never suffered in her forty years.
Her faith in Providence had been too great; and the
elements of sorrow had evaporated from her, leaving
but certain lines to mark the lack. She was as neat
as a church, and as quick as the wrath of God.

Now into the ear of this godless child, Hepzibah
plotted something to whisper; and for the results
thereof she would modestly, but firmly, claim her reward in heaven.

She supposed he was hungry. She advised him to
feel right at home, and not act bashful-like.

"Thanks very much; I will," said Gerald, studying
her face with polite composure. "Please may I see
your little pigs?"

"You c'n wait t'l ye 'v e't, can't ye? 'Member how
the Lodd druv the evil sperrits int' the bawdies of
swine, don't ye?" said Hepzibah, as a test.

"Yes," said the young person in knickerbockers;
"but I don't believe that. I think some bees mus'
have stinged them — stang them. And then they
went in swimming. Papa Zander sent his compli-
ments. He bought me a splendid fis'-line. I 'll go
and see the little pigs after I 've had something to
eat."

But when he had eaten the western sky was shot with
gold, and in the tangled garden the myriad petunias
and pansies and maiden pinks had gone to sleep. He
made a nosegay, and put it in a vase on his bureau,
about half-way between the photographs of his parents.
It was a trifle nearer Violet's, because you must favor

the women. Then he sat oppressed by the spare-room's gloom, while Jasper read Isaiah downstairs, and Hepzibah finished the dishes. He listened to the file of crickets' wings, and everywhere, in unison and out, the whistling of frogs; and the sounds were suggestive of night-damp and of disasters lurking for Mama Violet and Papa Zander. Hepzibah came to say good night, and then departed, leaving the room in a fog. He must hurry to use Mama Violet's home-sick medicine — to keep repeating *heimweh*, German; *mal-du-pays*, French; and the Italian *ché patisce la nostalgia*,— and thus cheat the blues of a language lesson. And he must remember that it was only two nights and a day; then he would meet Mama Violet's train at the station, and they would journey on to find Papa Zander. Besides, to-morrow would bring the fishing, at the beautiful pool, down beneath the willows.

He blew out the feeble lamp and crawled between the damp sheets, with the fish-line in his hand. To-morrow at the pool was lovely to think of! But he wished he had Mama Violet's kiss.

He hung the line over the bedside, and shut his eyes, trying to feel himself lying on the mossy bank in the leaf-latticed sunlight, waiting for a fish. The line swung slowly to and fro in the dark, and the boy kept mournfully thinking in time to it — *heimweh, mal-du-pays, ché patisce la nostalgia!* — until all the words ran into one, and the line dragged, and the fingers loosened, and the little hook dropped on the floor.

To-morrow would be Sunday.

II

A PEWEE made its woodland sigh, suited to sunny weather; but a robin announced that it would rain. The boy threw back the blinds that had darkened the room. The day seemed glorious. Between the apple-trees across the road he could see down to the salt creek where emptied the water from the stream that made the fishing-pool. In the creek the tide was high and still, and a forest of oaks and spruce and ash was mirrored in it from its granite bank, where stretched along a garland of deep blue harebells, mingled with yellow St. John'swort. Beyond and away were dense green forests, and, far above them, the faint cawing that brings a sense of distance and of solitude, and the resin smell and the music of the pines.

How foolish had been the *heimweh* when there was fishing to-day down beneath the willows!

"Please, Uncle Jasper," said Gerald, as he sat at breakfast, raised to their level by a great Bible, "I wis' you would show me the exact spot where Papa Zander used to fis'— the place where papa made you — where," corrected the Boy, coloring, "you and he had a fi — *fuss* one Sunday about the Bible. I have a splendid fis'line, and splendid hooks."

"'T was jest one them times," explained Jasper, slowly, in answer to his wife, "when the good Lodd see fit to chasten the one He loved best. I wa'n't feelin' any tew pert."

"No," said the Boy, sympathetically, "after you were chastened you felt jus' like a wet rag. Papa

Zander says it was the *Lord's* day, but that it was n't the Lord's *day*. It was whether Lazarus was really dead, Aunt Hepzibah, or had an epilepsic fit and jus' thought so."

Jasper's mind seemed miles away. Hepzibah looked absently at the child.

" Aunt Hepzibah," said the Boy, at length attacking the silence, " this — this holy volume is very convenient."

" Don't s' pose you have one t' home ? " she said.

" O, yes. Papa says it 's an interesting book."

" *Dews* he ! S 'pose he takes good care 't you sha'n't read it ? "

" Well, I may have the firs' expurgated edition. He says someone *mus'* have publis'ed one — for young people."

" S 'pose *he* 'd let 'em exp'gate the good Lodd right out of it ! "

" O, no — the Lord 's all right," said the Boy. " But if he had to esplain me everything in the Bible he says he 'd die before he did. That 's what expurgate means ; it 's the only word ever Mama Violet could n't esplain me — it 's so long. But Papa Zander knew ! It 's Latin, you see ; *purgo*, I make short ; *expurgo*, I make extra short. And that's what ought to be done with the Bible."

Jasper and Hepzibah stared at each other ; and for some minutes Gerald listened to the ticking of the clock.

" I don't suppose you 'll have time to go fis'in with me to-day, Uncle Jasper," he essayed, at length. " I 'm going — "

"Yuss," said Hepzibah, "*you're* goin' t' meetin' 'long 'th us."

"Why — what?" said the Boy. "Is it Sunday?"

"I sh'd say 't was. 'Bout the first one 't ever happened, guess."

"O!" said the Boy, vainly searching Hepzibah's countenance. "If I'd known that, I should n't have come prepared to fis'. What a diffunce!"

He dragged himself upstairs and emptied his pockets. All he had come for was to fis', down beneath the willows; and now he must preen and be taken off in the broiling sun. If after church he spoke of digging for worms it was plain that Aunt Hepzibah would have a fit. It was for this then that he had fought off *heimweh;* and now there was to be another night. Life was full of hardships, and the Bennett homestead was losing its charm. He heard the ancient pump yielding water with rusty and crabbed complaints, and Polly, the mare, drank with a swigging noise very ill-bred. The bell of the Hard Pine Methodists and that of the Cedar Creek Baptists were jarring and clashing across the narrow stream between them, over their respective creeds. If a little boy came to visit Papa Zander and Mama Violet, thought Gerald, perspiring over his collar-button, *he* would n't be hauled off to a meeting-house and expected to sit up stiff in a wooden pew! Would it be right to steal away this afternoon and quietly exploit the historic pool? It would be awful fun; but perhaps Mama Violet would say it was n't very polite and may be Papa Zander would think it was n't quite frank; and it would be a sort of fib, too — one of those you don't tell, but do,

which is just as bad. He wished he had stayed with
Papa Zander!

Of course there were clouds coming over the sun,
and the atmosphere was growing miserably humid.
Jasper was attaching Polly to the wagon.

"I don't suppose you'll go if it rains," said the Boy
with a faint hope, waving towards the threatening sky.

"Never missed it 'n ten years," said Jasper; "nor
Hepzibah 'n twenty."

"But if it rains awful hard, so hard that umbrellas
and mackintos'es and everything won't keep you dry,
what do you do?"

"We git wet," said Jasper.

They wedged him, hot and wretched, in between
them, and with a "Git up, Pawley — dew!" they
started off. "'Pawley'!" sniffed the Boy to himself.
What a horse! An abbreviation of polygon — irregular, meandering, knock-kneed polygon!

"See that long man comin' up the road," said Hepzibah. "That's Cory Judd. He's a very gawdless man, 'n' he never goes t' meetin' except when he
wants to, 'n' he's been known to catch fish of a Sunday. He won't never go to heaven, but is most likely
to be biled and pickled!"

"My!" said the Boy. "What a long pickle he'd
make!. But it won't hurt when he's dead, will it?"

"'T aint his bawdy, 't's his soul — his immortal
paht."

"But I thought a soul was jus' air? Do you think
Papa Zander will be pickled?"

"Them that mawks the Lodd must breathe fiuh 'n'
brimstun hereafter," said Hepzibah, solemnly.

"But," said the Boy, innocently quoting Mama Violet, "you can't accept that sort of a thing nowadays unless you throw your brains overboard."

The elders appeared not to have heard him, and he took to examining the approaching figure of Cory Judd.

"O," he said, suddenly, with as much breath as he could get, "I know Cory Judd! One time he and papa were boys. And they took some of the — the underpins from the school-house one night when they were having a fuss inside about the minister, and Mr. Judd and papa teetered the school-house, and Aunt Hepzibah ran out and said the Lord had sent an earthquake."

Uncle Jasper astonished the Boy with a burst of laughter.

"Howdy dew, Cory," said Jasper, as they drew up under a willow, and the Boy sighed. "Jest heard who 't was teetered the school-h'us'. You 're a sly one, you be; but I allus suspected ye, blast if I ain't! See — that was twenty years ago, come punkin-time, wa 'n't it? O, I say, Cory, kinder like t' use your hay-press little t' mawrer; mine 's bust. I — "

Mr. Judd had been regarding Hepzibah quizzically, recalling with great satisfaction the spectacle of her flight from the school-house twenty years ago.

"I allus knowed 't was you that teetered the school-h'us'!" she exclaimed. "You allus was a gawdless man, 'n' you allus will be. Don't misdoubt but what you 're goin' fishin' now!"

Mr. Judd stood with his great hand on the muddy tire of the wagon-wheel; he smiled faintly, and then pretended to erase the smile, and pulled a fish-line from his pocket.

"I 'm goin' to hang that there hook int' the water, where 't belawngs," he began to drawl nonchalantly, stopping at frequent intervals to spit. "Then I 'm goin' t' kinder set 'n' callate a while 'bout how the Lodd come to make Hepzibah Bennett. Now 'f any fish comes a-flandanderin round that there worm 'n' interferin' 'th my callations, why,—I shall callate to haul him out ont' dry tarritory, where such an inconsid'rate fish belawngs. For I callate that them what puts their noses int' what it ain't no pa't or pa'cel of them, why that they had ought to be somethin' did to!"

"S' pose you knowed 't was the Lodd's day," said Hepzibah, watching for an opening.

"So 's the hull seven."

"S'pose you knowed what the good book says."

"Yuss; but I 'm pestered 'f I know what it means more 'n half the time; nor you neither; nor them that goes t' Cedar Creek."

"Cedar Creek!" said Hepzibah, scornfully. "'F you 'd walk reg'lar t' hear the gawspel, 'stead of actin' like you was half-fuddled, mebbe you 'd get nearer the Lodd's meanin'."

"Huh!" said Cory, with a show of feeling. "I cal'late when I 'm out 'n the sawlitude, a-listenin' to His music in the woods, I 'm a dahn sight nearer the Lodd 'n ever you be, Hepzibiah. I don't perk up perpendicular 'n a pew, thinkin' plawts against the minister, b' gawsh!"

"Git up, Pawley!" cried Hepzibah. "I won't listen to no sech profanity."

Polly scrambled off in a scandal; and the Boy, twisting around, saw Cory grinning in the middle of the road. The Boy smiled back, then hove a tremendous sigh. Cory, regardless of the coming rain, was starting across the fields toward the willows.

"You need n't be a-smirkin', Jahsper Bennett," said his wife; "you ain't any tew blameless a man."

"Yes," retorted Jasper, flushing, "'n' how 'bout that hay press?"

The people with whom they fell in surmised who the little boy was with the great red bow. He had wavy hair, like Alexander's, and probably he was being trained in the light-heartedness for which his father was remembered. Hepzibah had never allowed Coosac to forget that Alexander and Violet Bennett were, to her belief, beyond salvation, except by a special dispensation which Hepzibah could never conscientiously endorse; but everybody knew why she kept Jasper asking for a visit from the Boy,—and her designs. So that they all craned to see him, and Hepzibah made various remarks to Jasper which showed how well she understood the shortcomings of the various members of the Hard Pine congregation.

The storm waited for the sermon, which was on the severe responsibility entailed by the possession of a soul. Then came lightning and thunder, growing apace with the force of the pastor's discourse. Whenever he pounded the desk a flash of lightning sprang ready from the heavens to drive his point home to the hearts of the sinners present. Deacon Stubb rose to close the blinds; and the one he left open to illuminate the desk, shutting the window against the rain, touched the face of the pastor with a gray glamour, very impressive when alternated with the lightning. Things were being said about renegades from the teachings of their youth, and how their sins should be weighted on their blood even to the third and fourth dilutions. Hepzibah watched the Boy, and many of the congregation looked at him and nodded from time to time at the pastor's words. The little girl who sat alone next Gerald, turned often to examine him, with approval mixed with regret, at what was gossiped. She was the Debney girl, and her people were sick. They were always sick, complained Hepzibah, with suspicion. The little girl was nervous, and frightened at the thunder. She was older than Gerald; but it was nicer to sit close to him than to hug the division of the pews. The Boy had been lost in an envious memory of Mr. Judd, and in self-demand whether he might in any propriety wander off to the pool after dinner. He had to conclude that, though Aunt Hepzibah would not care if she did not know, it would still be a sort of fib. Now he emerged from his reverie and grew absorbed in the pastor's control of the lightning, and in wondering what the effect would be if at the critical point the thunder should fail. The little girl was earnestly seeking for reassurance about the thunderbolts. Some of the older females turned anxiously in their seats, too; for the raging noise without was the wildest for years, and it became louder and louder, as if advancing directly upon the meeting-house. But Hepzibah sat in faith born of a clean soul, and in pride that the Spinney faction — those who upheld the present minister — should ob-

10

serve the son of Alexander brought to the Hard Pine Meeting-house. Then came a tremendous flash of lightning, accompanying the most solemn thing the pastor had said with a simultaneous and deafening report of thunder that told for the church a narrow escape. There was a creaking without and a great gust, which brought the huge branch of a stately elm down with a thump against the building. The service was broken in; for two women had fainted, and several others were panic-stricken and wished to flee, they knew not whither; and the three small daughters of one of those who had swooned broke into tears. There was talking, as the men tried to reassure the women; and Elzira Spinney, who was never more frightened than Hepzibah Bennett, fastened her eyes upon Gerald, and said aloud:

"The judgment of the Lodd is on the evil—'n' on them of their blood."

And Deacon Stubb, who sided with Hepzibah, and was the coolest man in the church because he could not hear thunder, and knew only by the movement of the lips what was said, replied reverently:

"The Lodd chasteneth them he loveth."

The Boy had sat dazed by the close embrace of the little girl. The two had stared speechlessly into each other's eyes for a whole minute. Then he recovered, remembering the victory at the fishing-pool years ago, and said:

"It's all right. The Lord won't chasten *me*."

"Sh—!" said Hepzibah, angrily, glancing to see if Elzira had noticed. Elzira had. She was as good as Hepzibah, so many people thought.

"But Elziry means you," said the little girl, clinging to him, as another sharp crash came, from apparently as near as the others. "Your father is a heathen. Ain't you scared?"

"Oh, no," said the Boy, audibly above the sobbing of the three little girls across the church. "If Papa Zander were here, he 'd jus' make a speech, and I guess the lightning would go away. He did it once when there was a fire at a theater, and it went out."

"But—oh!" cried the little girl, blinded by the next flash, which was as brilliant but less severe,— "how do you know but what the Lodd's mad because you came to meetin'?"

"Well, he could n't hit me without hitting you," said the Boy in unconscious criticism of her attitude. "Anyway, you 'd get struck by the pieces, and he would n't do that."

"Keep still, can't ye!" cried Hepzibah, angrily, giving him a vigorous shake, and casting sheep's eyes around the church. The Boy's face paled. He had never been handled in his life. He looked up quickly at his aunt with quivering nostrils. The organ had begun the doxology. The service was being cut short on account of the sisters who had fainted.

Hepzibah hastened from the sanctuary, and they drove off at once, under the single cotton umbrella, before any one could detain them.

"Don't ye know 't ye should n't tok out 'n the Lodd's house that way!" exclaimed Hepzibah, as soon as they were out of hearing, in the manner she might have used to her own child, if she had been a mother. "It don't become one of your breedin' t' make free 'n the house of Gawd!"

"That little girl was afraid," said Gerald, gasping

from the pressure of their bodies; "and I jus' *told* her."

"Don't make no diff'runce. Had n't ought to opened your mouth. Tokkin' 'bout theaters 'n' sech-like, I never 'n all my bo'n days! What 'll Elziry Spinney say? Ain't you got no trainin' at all? I sh think you was a cannibal!"

"I 'm not a cannibal!" retorted the Boy, miserably. "I don't like you, Aunt Hepzibah — I don't! I wish I had never seen you! I want to go home."

"Sh' think you would," snuffed Hepzibah, unrelent-ingly. "Ain't comf'table with the upright-minded, be ye? Want t' git back t' Alexander, 'n' cahd-playin', theater-goin', 'n' all the sins of creation, don't ye? Your father 's a gawdless man, 'n' your mother tew, 'n' it 's my dooty before the Lodd to tell ye so!"

"My papa 's the best man in the world!" cried the Boy, flaming with rage; "and my mama — O, I hate you! Her little finger 's a million times better than you! I 'll tell her you shook me, and she 'll never let you look at me, even if I wanted to. I *hate* you!" he iterated, struggling with tears, and fighting to be up and away from her.

"Your father ——" began Hepzibah, slowly and dis-tinctly.

"'Ll there now, Hep," said Jasper, with sudden firmness, "you got t' stawp, d' ye hear?"

"Jahsper Bennett!" exclaimed Hepzibah, with her look.

"I say 't you got t' stawp right this minute," said Jasper, meeting her eyes with astonishing self-asser-tion. "I don't want t' hear 'nother word. Aleck 's

my brother — he ain't yourn. You ain't got the *hull*
world ont' your shoulders, not by a long sight; 'n'
you *tok too much!* Git up, Pawley!"

He took the Boy on his knee and lashed Polly into
a hurry. The boy kept sniffing and looking ahead of
him, pale in the face. The sun was peeping through
the clouds; the day was on again, and the red-winged
blackbirds were trilling in the swamps. The dim beds
of pine spills in the thick grove under the hill looked
as brown and dry as if it had never rained. It must
be fresh and sweet down under the willows now,
thought the Boy, with a wretched gulp at the prospects for until to-morrow. Dear Mama Violet!

At dinner Jasper tried to be entertaining. Hepzibah was silent. The boy would not look at her; and
what Jasper said was interesting to boys of six, perhaps, but not to boys of eight. Jasper did n't sug-
gest a walk, because he thought the grass too wet.
Hepzibah was considering, and concluding that this
child must be handled with policy. Elzira Spinney
had brought people to church that way and converted
them, pretending at first to tolerate many graceless
things. Hepzibah had a new idea.

"You c'n have this old Bible, little boy," she said.
"You c'n read it; 'n' if Violet says anything, you tell
her *I* said so. What you don't understand you jest
come t' me."

"I think I 'll read it in my room," said the Boy, not
looking her in the eye, and driven to the first artifice
of his life. He wanted to be alone and to decide
whether such unusual circumstances did not warrant
his quiet departure for the pool, when the elders had

10*

arranged themselves for the afternoon. They would n't mind if they did n't know ; and the Lord would n't mind if he did know. At least, if he would, he would have blasted Cory Judd that very day, down beneath the willows !

Perhaps he had. Suppose Mr. Judd was lying there now with a great rift from head to toe, such as Gerald had seen in tree trunks ? He might be stretched out stiff on the mossy bank with the fis'-line grasped in his hand; and perhaps there was a little fis' tugging at the end of the dead man's line. The Boy wondered if it was not his duty to go down and see. For though their lines had fallen in different waters since, Papa Zander and Mr. Judd had once been playmates.

Could he climb down the corner-post of the porch over the main door ? Of course he had but to step out on the roof. The front room down-stairs was never used except for weddings and funerals. But there was Hepzibah coming up. He sat pretending to read the book she had given him. That was right, said Hepzibah ; she would see that he was not disturbed. She went out and closed the door. Then she locked it.

Here was a new and extraordinary aggravation, thought the Boy. Of course he could escape to the brook by the window, but that would still be a sort of fib. He drew a great breath — it was a weighty question. If he remained, there was nothing to do but read the Bible, which was a matter of doubtful propriety ; for though Papa Zander had never said so, it was plain enough that both he and Mama Violet considered the book hardly one for young boys. And if you knew that, it was no excuse to say that you had n't been told in so many words. If he went fis'ing, why, papa might not approve of that, and there would be such a fuss with Aunt Hepzibah ! Yet, after all the miseries of the day, it was simply too much to expect him to sit still. Finally he decided on the Bible.

Hepzibah had inserted a card at that page of Revelation which reveals the final destiny of the unbelieving and the abominable end of several exceedingly objectionable classes of persons. The Boy disregarded this verse of the lake of fire, and turned at random to another part. He had heard of people who thus discovered what to do for their woes. He looked where his finger had struck, and read, in the eighth verse of the thirty-third chapter of Deuteronomy :

"And of Levi he said : Let thy Thummim and thy Urim be with thy holy one."

"'Thy Thummim and thy Urim'?" he repeated. "I wonder—? Dear, I wis' Papa Zander was here! Now I shall never be happy until I know all about thy Thummim and thy Urim ; and may be if I had waited for my expurgated edition I should n't have known anything about it!"

In the midst of this he heard a voice which seemed familiar, singing with studied carelessness a quaint refrain of which the air of the first two lines was the same with that of the last two. The words were :

> Heart-weed and smart-weed,
> They look just the same ;
> And ye could n't tell 'em 'part—
> If it was n't for their names!

or, as Cory Judd improved them:

> Ha 't-weed 'n' sma't weed
> 'Ey look jest a-same 's
> Ye could n't tell 'em 'pa't
> 'F 'twa' n't for th' names!

Cory was making a dumb show. The Boy understood with delight.

"Letter for ye," he whispered, with a wave. "Did n't
want t' git Hepzy a-vaporin' at me. Kinder mistrusted
you was Aleck's boy. S' pose I could git this up to ye
'thout sta'tin' Hepzy?"

The Boy thought so; he ran and got the new fish-
line and let it down from the roof of the porch.

"Son of Aleck, b' George," said Cory, putting the
hook through the corner of the envelope. "Come
last night down t' the station; Foster give it to me
this noon."

He wanted to know if Aleck was still getting rich
and whether Violet was as handsome as ever — which
the Boy was positive she was. Was the Boy going
fishing to-morrow? No? There followed explana-
tions, and a history of the day, told with moderate
reference to Hepzibah. Well, was the Boy going to
stay cooped up in the spare room, or did he think of
sliding down and going fishing, same 's Aleck would
have?

"I don't know," said the Boy, hopelessly. "You see,
it *would* be a sort of fib, and if she asked me, I 'd have
to tell, and then —!"

"Ay, yuss," allowed Cory, but with some show of
disappointment. "Still, I dunno 's that would have

hindered Aleck in his day, leastwise — but it hain't for
me t' meddle. By! I 'm goin' down along. Did n't
have no tho't of fishin' this mo'nin', jest said so t'
please Hepzy."

He saw Cory brushing through the moist field, safe
from the range of Hepzibah's windows. The quick
kingbirds were darting at the grasshoppers; a cool,
fresh breeze was nodding the daisies, and the butter-
flies fluttered in the sun. But there was nothing but
the Bible for a virtuous little boy. "'Thy Thummim
and thy Urim'!" he repeated, with an access of woe.
Hot tears filled his eyes, and his fists contracted,—
until he remembered the letter.

It was from Papa Zander! It had been jotted on
the train, and that was what made papa's hand look
so foreign. Really, except Mama Violet, there was
nothing in the world like Papa Zander!

A song-sparrow sang charmingly afield. The Boy
sat by the window with his elbows on the table. The
red bow was where it had worked askew when he had
tried to escape from Hepzibah; and his hair was
tumbled with his search for the meaning of Thummim and Urim — a search still vain among theologi-
ans. But he was feeling better. As he read, his face
grew brighter and brighter, and he smiled to himself.
He was too excited to notice that Hepzibah had come
and quietly unlocked the door and silently gone away.
Finally he laughed aloud.

He jumped up and pocketed the fish-line and the
big field-knife that belonged to Alexander. Then he
stepped out on the roof of the porch. All was clear.
If it was n't clear, no matter. Mr. Judd had disap-

peared, but there was the happy, winding path. The Boy slid with stout little limbs down the post and walked in a straight line towards where the path cut the birches and undergrowth. If Hepzibah looked up at the right moment she would surely see him; but if you think you are right you don't have to dodge.

The letter lay open on the table.

ALEXANDER M. BENNETT,
　　Attorney-at-Law.

MEMORANDUM.

On the train.

Dear little Thumpty-bump:

Papa neglected to warn you that your aunt and uncle hold different views from yours, especially about Sunday. But all people are to be respected for what they sincerely believe. If you went fishing on Sunday, Aunt Hepzibah would say you were a bad little boy; and though you are always a good boy, it would not be *poli* to argue with her. But it is not a case where because you are a child you are obliged to subscribe to beliefs you may reject when you are older. I do not know what you think about fishing on Sunday, but so far as you are responsible for what you do, it is on account of what you know and believe. Be sure you are right and then go ahead — if you think it right to go ahead. If Aunt Hepzibah asks questions, answer them with your usual frankness, but so as not to wound the lady who is entertaining you so kindly.

You will find two dear little orchids in the swamp back of the pool. They are *arethusa* and *calopogon;* but they might have been anæsthesia and paregoric for all I knew until I was three times your age. One of them smells as dainty-sweet as a fairy's smelling-bottle. There are apt to be wood-warblers, too, pecking at the trunks and leaves of the willows — they like the older ones with the bright yellow lichens. Make yourself akin with nature, my boy, and you will never be far from whatsoever God may mean.

If you see Mr. Cory Judd — you won't find him at meeting — tell him papa has not forgotten the little red school-house and the earthquake.

Surely be on time to take care of Mama Violet.

Your very affectionate

PAPA.

P. S. *I* used to think they bit better on Sundays. They did n't suspect.   Papa.

N. B. I used to hang *mine* in the hollow of a tree until Monday.   Papa.

"Maybe Mr. Judd knows about thy Thummim and thy Urim!" thought the Boy, skipping gaily through the fragrant shrubbery.

III

THE Monday morning train rolled up to the little Coosac flag-station, with Mama Violet expectant at the open window of the parlor car.

"There she is! There she is, Mr. Judd!" said the Boy, breaking away from the grasp of Hepzibah, who had no belief in steam-cars. "Hello, mama! Hello, mama! Is n't she lovely, Mr. Judd? Good-by, Aunt Hepzibah. Good-by, Uncle Jasper! Good-by, Mr. Judd! Hope we 'll meet again, Mr. Judd,— when you come to Boston."

The Boy dashed up the steps of the car and ran in to find Mama Violet. He encircled her neck with both arms, and nearly smothered her with kisses.

"He 's a pretty *sma't* boy," allowed Hepzibah from the platform. "Got up this mo'nin' 'for' *we* was up, 'n' cot three suckers 'n' three them little trout down t' the brook."

At this statement Mr. Cory Judd slapped his knee and went into an almost dangerous fit of laughter.

"No I did n't," called the Boy, as the train moved quickly out. "I shinned down and caught them yesterday, and, Aunt Hepzibah,— *kept them in a tree!*"

But Hepzibah was saying at the same time as loud as she could:

"I took him to meetin', 'n' I give him a Bible, Violet, 'n' I set him ont' the path of grace. 'F you don't see t' the rest of his salvation, *that be on your soul!*"

Sweet Violet, with her son's hand tight in hers, looked back on the lady of the Hard Pine Meeting-house and smiled. The Boy wriggled up close to her and put his arm around her waist.

"O don't let 's ever part again, mama! She shook me and made me read the Bible because I told the little girl the lightning would n't kill her. And I went fis'ing — it *was* a kind of fib; but I told Aunt Hepzibah jus' now. But the pool was the loveliest place! And warblers and annethusias, and Mr. Judd! He's the funniest Mr. Judd you ever saw, but he did n't know,— mama, what is thy Thummim and thy Urim? Mama, did you get my book: 'How Monkeys Speak?' O, mama, darling, don't let us *ever* part again so long as we live!"

THE TRAGEDY OF THE COMEDY

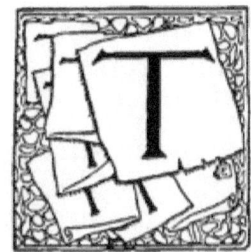HEY crisped the snow of Boston Common dressed in handsome fabrics, carrying themselves as some princesses do and as every princess should. Their waists, within the easy embrace of their bodices, were free and supple, as God planned. The winter air bit their cheeks.

Charlotte was strongly boned. Her face was full and her mouth was large and firm, its smile endowed with liberal range of meaning. Her eyes were of the North — blue and quiet. Jessica was an inch taller, a woman with fine frame and slender hands. Her feet were small, but capable of much ground. Her eyes were like the Italian sky. Her face was pale, with the pure, high, narrow brow that sculptors choose. Both girls had chestnut-glossy hair, and both were twenty-eight years old. One would have thought them twenty-four.

They had been walking steadily for four hours. It was visible that Charlotte and Jessica were different from other girls. They were as well groomed as women of fashion. Their faces had the dignity and cast of thought of the fostered intellect, but not the postgraduate air of abstraction; nor did the girls bear the trivial weights of the mode.

Charlotte pressed with her elbow a book, thinking of the story in its pages, written by her friend Mr. Bond. She could not help marveling at his genius.

Jessica, seeing into her friend's mind, noticed with a twinge how the volume was affectionately handled by Charlotte. Jessica was silent until the pressure became too great. Then she began:

"You did n't believe, a year ago, that to-day his name would stand so high."

"No," said Charlotte, accustomed to these interpretations. "At least I did n't believe he would achieve this. I confess I thought he might succeed in something ingenious, or perhaps humorous, or fantastic; but not that he was equal to this sort of thing. I don't think we ever overestimated him," she added.

"After all, though," said Jessica, "a single fairish novel does not confer immortality. Heaven knows that some of the stuff printed might have been written by you or me."

"I said that to Mr. Bond once, and he asked me if I had ever entered into any competition for money."

"Implying that you were a babbling infant. That was quite like him," said Jessica, with a short laugh.

"He was right. I don't know why you should forever disparage him — after all this time," said Charlotte, with dignity.

"I have no pedestal for Mr. Bond," said Jessica. "I don't think I ever pretended otherwise."

"Not to him, surely — or me!"

"Oh, I suppose you 'll marry him in the end," said Jessica, bitterly.

Charlotte would not answer. A flush came over

Jessica's face. They walked on, looking far ahead, until they entered the Public Garden. There Jessica stopped abruptly and whirled around.

"You know you love him — and are sorry!" she said passionately.

Charlotte slowly raised her eyes to Jessica.

"If ever I do — I will tell you before I tell him, dear," she said.

"And that will part us forever. You know it," said Jessica, wretchedly. "You know I never cared for any one in the world but you. But you have forgotten all you once felt."

"You have charged me with that so often," said Charlotte, deprecatingly, "and you know it is not true. Why should we reopen that miserable, impossible subject?"

"And we used to agree that we should so like the same man that it would be an outrage on the other for either of us to marry him," continued Jessica, in a tone that implied absolute foreknowledge of an event.

"If you refer by chance to Mr. Bond, you know you could have liked him if you had wished to."

"Yes; you still think I am jealous of him — or of you," said Jessica.

"How absurd! I cannot forget, though, that you spoke of him with more enthusiasm than I did, at first."

"That was because I did not want to marry him."

"Jessica, you are childish. I did not want to marry him."

"No; but you are going to."

11

Charlotte said nothing. They were at their own door. They parted to dress for the evening.

THESE girls had met at college. Their strange hypersensitiveness and its concurrent melancholy had immediately joined them together. Their friendship grew to one of those affairs not infrequent in women's colleges. It was not the ordinary intimacy between girls; it was peculiar and binding. It formed a creed around itself — one which came to regulate almost every action of their lives. They rose together, ate together, studied together, and walked together. To Jessica, Charlotte was a Juno, fearless and born to rule. To Charlotte, Jessica was a flower of surpassing gentleness, made to be cherished and directed. Their tastes were identical, and their capabilities were the wonder of those years with their alma mater. They did not affect a special trend, but sipped of every stream which pleased their fancy and widened their touch with realms of science and pure imagination. They entered little into the social circles of student life, passing their time rather in voracious readings, both of books and nature. They knew every flower and bit of stone and creeping or flying thing the country round. Both were independent in money, though no bait for fortune-seekers, and both delved well below the surface of all that excited their interest, purely for the satisfaction that is dilettante.

As each year tightened their friendship they saw less and less of other girls, and cared less for the society of men. They contrived reasons for not going home during the recess, in order that they might spend the time more closely together. When their relatives rebelled, the girls parted in gloom, and wrote letters regularly every day until they came back early to the college walls.

The most serious incident in their college career, except the friendship itself, followed upon the suggestion of the lady professor of French to the lady principal, that the two girls were taking too morbid an interest in each other, and should be kept more apart, for the good of their minds and the moral benefits of occasional solitude. Charlotte and Jessica packed their belongings and wrote long letters home, which resulted in the lady principal's relenting, while the lady professor of French shrugged her shoulders. The girls altered their course from French to Spanish.

When they left college Charlotte immediately came to Boston to live with Jessica and Jessica's father and brothers. Jessica had been motherless for several years, and Charlotte had lost both her parents during her course at college. In Boston their life went on again in much the same channels, only at first more delightfully than ever; for the girls were free to go wherever they pleased. They saw, heard, and read everything that was well played or sung or written; and the brilliant cynicism which grew gradually out of their view and mode of life afforded them now a regular pleasure in averting the attentions of successive men, some of them mediocre and fatuous, a few superior to the girls, but all with traits that made them interesting for the time, and all subjected to the cold, critical spirit not rare in clever modern women who have never allowed themselves in competition or in true fellowship with the sturdier sex.

Many men passed in review through their drawing-rooms for the amusement of the girls, but few made more than half a dozen visits. This was apt to be the extent of their true welcome, and generally sufficed to convey a subtle impression on the men quite suited to the circumstance. Humor of a high quality, and much wit and flippancy, the girls received with applause; but it was painful to fall below their standard, and those who talked of serious matters were chilled by the lack of enthusiasm of the girls, which seemed to express a complete disapproval of masculine ideals. Those who survived these conditions were either entertaining creatures unconscious of themselves, or else men who fancied themselves in love with one of the girls, in the fashion of male creatures for so long as there have been scintillant beings in the world about whom a man may build a domestic halo in his imagination. These latter men were the greatest sport of all, unless Jessica, to whom they did not often attach themselves, began to draw a fear from Charlotte's really gentler manner that Charlotte's heart was in absurd danger of being touched. Jessica then disposed of the enemy in a way that was at once humane and expeditious in the hands of the lady of the house; and Charlotte made no sound, though she would have been interested in a more extended observation of the inferior animal when it lost its sentimental balance. The two often laughed together over subsequent wedding-cards engraven with the names of the departed and of sweet young things.

But there came Mr. Bond, who was a minor officer in the city government. The girls took him as the greatest curiosity, and Jessica viewed him as wholly harmless because he had scanty means, and no future except in his aspirations to a literary career. He explained this to them, and they received it kindly, because it seemed pathetic that one with so narrow an education compared to theirs, a man who told them in the triumph of discovery many a thing they had read in the ancient philosophers, should be possessed of his hopes. But Bond had two qualifications which they overlooked, perhaps without blame. He was constantly making the most astounding acquaintances with his own shortcomings, which he confided to them as if he had been an insect under his own microscope; and he was constantly drawing a larger interest on this knowledge of himself — all this with a persistence in the face of certain odds that would have inspired the girls if they had not been so nearly content with their spiritual condition. One might have inferred from them that he was illiterate; but he was far from that: his obstacles were great only when measured from the goal he had set for himself, and when it was understood how little leisure he had. But the girls looked to him mainly for amusement, and for an agreeable outlet for easy-going charity, rather than for the inspiriting current of sympathy that may flow between the sexes. He was always diving into some unexpected corner and producing some extraordinary character in the flesh, or some outlandish inanimate thing that was new to them, and hence highly exciting. And with all his youthful ardor, as they said it, he had a certain dignity, such

11*

that they could not feel toward him as they did toward any other man.

They did not both perceive, as they knew him better, that while he seemed to look to them for instruction in his spiritual growth, referring continually to their opinions, he constantly made progress in a direction of which he was sole arbiter. In time Charlotte felt it; but Jessica forever ignored that he had views that were to be taken seriously, or were in touch with the times.

They had begun to honor him with invitations to show them curious corners in Boston, when Jessica, much against her choice, was constrained to go abroad with her father, in tardy response to his request made before she went to college. And it happened that property complications and a lawsuit of importance required Charlotte's presence at a town on the Maine coast, where her people had made their all in the rise of summer-resort real estate. When Jessica was halfway across the Atlantic, and heavy with the journal of three days' longings for Charlotte, Mr. Bond was taking Charlotte for walks on the cliff at Seaweed Cove.

It was during this miserable period of cathedrals and homesickness for Charlotte that Jessica began to dream how Mr. Bond might become a dangerous possibility. Charlotte, she considered, was, after all, entirely too susceptible to men, and would, if left to herself, be apt to take them to heart. Besides, Charlotte was excessively charming to contemplate — she could do anything in the world, from making a Greek verse to making a creamed lobster; and Charlotte was not alert to know that what men said to her was always with an ulterior purpose — that of putting the girl in wedding-harness, with all that sort of humble reality so reverse from the silly dreams of young creatures who have not learned that the best philosophy confers a higher title on friendship than it does on love. "Clingers" was Jessica's favorite designation for girls who confessed to a certain moral support exerted by men. Jessica herself was of the "clinger" order, but in a perverted and most exaggerated form, and this was the secret of her adhesion to Charlotte. As much as she admired Charlotte's self-reliance, she feared it because it was always dangerously near an independence quite opposed to the theory of their bonded lives.

Meanwhile, with cliffs and sea, and conversation over the field of human aspirations, Charlotte came into a new and delightful world that fascinated her and appealed to her most healthy sentiments. She enjoyed herself in a fashion which Jessica would have trembled to see, and did weep over when it was described in Charlotte's letters with many appreciative items concerning Mr. Bond. Charlotte spent hours and hours in the sunlight, sitting silent while Bond descanted on various subjects, arriving in the end, with unerring aim, at a chosen center. If they began to talk of fish in the sea, he made some remark about the jewfish, then about the patriarchal system of Jewish life, then about family life in general, then about the married life of young people. If they spoke of rocks, he would draw her out concerning mineralogy and crystals and jewels, and would tell her of a remarkable wedding-ring he had seen, and recount an anecdote of its wearer, from which he would draw deductions of an abstract nature. If they started on sand and seaweed, he straightway wondered under what circumstances the poet happened on the simile of the sands of time and the footprints thereon; then talked about poets, and Longfellow in particular, and Longfellow's ideal married life. Then he talked of his own future and apologized unceasingly for his failings in the deeper sort of culture, which seemed to her to lie in the direction of material, rather than in the lack of imagination or feeling. He spoke of a little book on which he was secretly at work — to be published by and by at his own expense; and she half gave her approval to its plan, though it did not seem quite in keeping with all the rest she thought of him. Then he announced to her that he was going abroad in another week as agent for a new steam-valve, and might not return too soon, unless she desired it for her special benefit. This was at the end of two months, and after three days' trepidation, in thought of what Jessica would say to all this, Charlotte finally gave way, and they confided in her aunt.

The aunt smiled, and reserved her opinion for a better acquaintance with the gentleman — which she never obtained, since the young people were always out of reach; until at length Mr. Bond went away, leaving Charlotte blue and happy, then blue and wishing for Jessica's return, then blue and doubtful. And Mr. Bond and Jessica passed on the ocean, Jessica with a cablegram in her pocket-book, and sunken to the depths of melancholy that her Charlotte should stoop to matrimony at all, not to speak of the abominable choice of a wretched steam-valve novelist whose culture could be stowed away comfortably in the minutest corner of Charlotte's brain; a man, thought Jessica, who would shine, if he ever did, solely by reflected light, and in miserable lesser ways that would be forever a shame and humiliation.

So Jessica made up her mind that the engagement should be declared off as soon as she could reach Charlotte, which would be on the pier at New York. The two went to their hotel and wept together for a number of hours, and Jessica assumed a superior attitude that was altogether fresh to her, first searching Charlotte's soul, and then engaging in an analysis of Mr. Bond that left him like a dried thing in a museum. Charlotte pleaded for him with no avail, for Jessica showed that he was neither an ardent student, nor an athlete, nor a linguist, nor a man of affairs — all of which symbolic utterances she amplified until they comprised every attribute which may possibly give a male creature the right of existence under any code of moral law. Moreover, she intimated that Mr. Bond would find Charlotte's money a welcome substitute for the traveling steam-valve, which was the only part of the inquisition where Charlotte frightened her friend with flashing of the eyes. Then Jessica attacked the institution of marriage on general grounds, and quoted so many of Charlotte's own cavils at it that Charlotte finally felt obliged to acknowledge her foolishness, and to write a note to Mr. Bond explaining what a grievous mistake she had made; that she did not love him, and could never marry him.

This was Bond's first serious experience in being misprized, and he careened so badly under the burden that he seemed quite to fit Jessica's estimate of him, and confirmed forever the abstractions concerning men made by Jessica out of her innocence of them. Mr. Bond wrote back that he regretted Charlotte had taken him for some other man. He filled four pages with shivering sarcasm that made Charlotte think Jessica much wiser than had been suspected by her most irresponsible admirers. For a year the matter seemed a closed incident.

During that year Mr. Bond continued his researches within himself, and finally came, in the light of a soul that grew constantly, to be heartily ashamed of his last communication to the woman he had loved and still loved. To arrive at such a state meant for him straightway to write another letter, proudly explaining his new understanding of his unworthiness, and telling of all the mental anguish he had undergone since they parted, and how completely he comprehended what his attitude must have stood for in her eyes. And Charlotte, moved, as she thought, by her conscience, replied that they both had much to regret, she especially in having allowed him to form such an impression of her regard for him, which had been, and would always be, simply that of a friend who admired his honesty and many other traits of his character. It turned out soon afterward that the steam-valve brought him back to Boston, and he called on Charlotte, and they took up the same friendly intercourse that had been the rule before he had ever touched on the subject of marriage.

This reconciliation was bitterly opposed by Jessica, and never gave her a moment's peace. But Charlotte stood like a rock, and went so far as to insist that Jessica should not forget the courtesy of a gentlewoman when Mr. Bond came in of an evening; to which Jessica yielded, though she came very near dangerous ground on more than one occasion. Mr. Bond informed Charlotte that he knew that he had forfeited much of her respect by his letter at the breaking of their engagement, but that he should not rest until he had regained what he had lost, and shown her that he was right when he said he could make her happy, which was a tremendous undertaking for any man in any circumstances, and stood for an optimism on his part that was an argument in itself.

So another year passed, during which the once ideal life of the two girls seemed to have permanently altered in a most distressing manner. They developed. They bickered over many things, all of which had root in Jessica's specter of Mr. Bond in eventual triumph; and as often as they bickered they wept and mutually asked forgiveness, though Charlotte would rarely accede to Jessica's demands for limitations on Mr. Bond's occurrence at the house. Mr. Bond had now become literary editor of a Boston daily, and smiled good-naturedly at his own small knowledge of the classics, ancient or modern, when he compared it to that of the girls. He even took the humor of Jessica's occasional causticity born of reading his reviews as the only side of her remarks worth appearing to notice; and meanwhile the paper increased his salary and gave him more space in the

Sunday edition, and other newspaper men looked upon him as a leader in his line. There grew a limit
to which Charlotte would listen to Jessica's sarcasms,
and henceforth Jessica never rose without bracing
herself for the announcement of an engagement; for
Charlotte became more silent every day.

The truth was that though Charlotte had said at
first it would be useless to look forward to any change
in her heart, her subsequent reception of his subtly
caressing tones had been such as to warrant a different belief. However, he resolved never to speak unless she showed conclusively that she wished him to.
And Charlotte, between the opposition of Jessica and
the expansion of her own womanly yearnings, came
into that region of feminine doubt which lets things
take care of themselves. For Charlotte was growing,
while Jessica stood still. And it finally happened
that on the eve of another of his departures from
Boston, Mr. Bond, finding his way by chance unan-
nounced into their drawing-room, came upon Charlotte standing at the mantelpiece, contemplating a
mask of Mirth.

Charlotte did not care anything for a mask of
Mirth; for her eyes were full of tears; and she could
not conceal them from him when she turned around.
But, unhappily, neither could she explain them; and
when he made a wise suggestion, she averred that she
could not truthfully say she loved him, and urged that
much the best way was for them to part indefinitely.
He then had his opportunity to cover the memory of
his first rejection with a manly speech. He said gently
that he should love her always, and that he would

wait patiently until she was ready, no matter how long it took. And he went off in a driving rain, leaving her in tears, as he had found her.

Jessica's imagination and artfulness extracted this much from mournful Charlotte the next day. Jessica then showed conclusively, on the highest moral grounds, that it was a grievous wrong to Mr. Bond for Charlotte to let him suppose she felt what she could not own to her dearest friend. And Charlotte, out of her affection for Mr. Bond, wrote to him that she was now sure that she would never marry him, though she omitted to say that she was sure that she did not love him. Mr. Bond did not write for a correction of this omission, for fear that, with the exaggerated notion of the truth which takes possession of fretful maids, she would supply it.

On the contrary, he wrote that he felt that Charlotte would in the end arrive at the point he desired; that he was aware of the antagonism of Miss Jessica, but that, after all, a regard weaker than objections external, and perhaps not wholly unselfish, would not justify any woman in entering matrimony; and that he was content to wait until Charlotte understood this. He said that Charlotte seemed constructed to prove that the first institution of our civilization could be a success for one who possessed her qualities; and he thereby came dangerously near complimenting himself, since he implied himself capable of supplying the other element for the triumph of his theory. He tried to state gently that Charlotte was spending the best years of her life in aimlessness, and that her constitutional tendency to melancholy would increase as

long as she refused to work out normally a scheme
of existence planned more for her benefit than for
that of anybody else in the world. He said that he
loved her, and expected her to discover that she loved
him, and that he should wait until she acknowledged it.

It was two years later when the girls were dining
in their new house after Jessica's outburst in the Public Garden. Jessica sulked. They were going to see
two comedies, one of which, in one act, had been written by Mr. Bond, and was now to be produced for the
first time in Boston, after a run in New York which
was announced as a success. When it was time for
the theater Jessica refused to go, despite the prayers of
Charlotte. So Charlotte left Jessica at home, and
went off with Jessica's brother.

As they sat waiting for the rise of the curtain, she
saw Mr. Bond enter one of the boxes, accompanied
by some ladies. He had changed considerably, perhaps for the better, she thought. He looked as old as
he was, and certainly could not convey that impression of youthfulness which went with his earlier days.
Charlotte watched him intently — the man who had
won her imagination to the only earthly career she
could now contemplate with a hope of happiness.
His manner seemed to have become graver. There
were a few streaks of premature gray in his hair.

Bond's comedy was the story of a girl who had sent
away the man who loved her. Now she regretted it,
but to no purpose, since from the occasional conven-
tional letters which passed between them she believed
that his heart had fallen into possession of another.

Soon the lover returned. There was a long scene in which she was caused to shadow forth her sorrow at his change of sentiment, ending with the announcement on his part that the other woman in the case was only a myth, and had been invented by him so that the girl might place a true value on what she thought she had lost. The letters were read over, and the description of the girl who did not exist was found to be that of the girl who did exist, and who now fell into the arms of the hero. This, after some little feminine difficulties were overcome, enabled the curtain to fall on hearts united.

As Mr. Bond left the box and passed along with the two ladies, Charlotte noticed that one of them was young and looked very clever and happy. She was evidently the daughter of the other lady. Bond caught sight of Charlotte, and hastened over to speak to her.

"What do you think of the girl in the play?" he asked, after the customary exchange.

"The girl gets more than she deserves," said Charlotte, brightly.

"In the play she does," said Bond.

"Shall you stay long in Boston?" asked Charlotte. She did not know what she might say next.

"No; I leave to-night — now that the little play seems to catch favor. Good-by."

He was gone.

"Bond is getting to be a notable," said Jessica's brother. "That was a fine-looking girl he had with him."

For Charlotte the second play dragged wofully.

The atmosphere seemed too heavy to breathe. She longed to be alone in the open air.

During these moments Jessica, at home, very unhappy, and ravishingly handsome in her evening gown, was making furious game of the admiring Chauncey Barber, the young medical student and religious enthusiast whose courage was apparent only by fits and starts. In the course of the evening he chanced to remark :

"That's a beauty Franklin Bond is going to marry, don't you think ?"

"Who ?" asked Jessica, excitedly.

Barber took revenge for her raillery by refusing to tell.

Later, when the girls were alone, they were both unusually gay. Charlotte soon pleaded fatigue, and retired to her room. Jessica went to sleep determined to find out at the earliest opportunity if Mr. Bond was betrothed.

When Charlotte awoke in the morning she was ill. As the day wore on she grew worse. Evening found the doctor at her bedside. The illness developed into typhoid fever. For weeks Jessica scarcely left Charlotte's chamber. She slept at Charlotte's side on a mattress on the floor, nursing her day and night. It was a great strain on the nerves of the more delicate girl; all the more from a fearful anxiety for Charlotte's life, which sometimes kept Jessica awake far toward the dawn, when she lay exhausted after a day of highest tension. In those hours Jessica went back over the history of their lives together, and blamed herself for many a childish jealousy over Charlotte, and for many a cutting speech born of unreasoning hatred of those occasional third persons who took Charlotte's fancy. Now Charlotte would forget Mr. Bond, if what Barber said was true. And the lives of the two girls, if death would only spare Charlotte, would go on, with Jessica chastened in spirit, and risen to a new dignity, through the loveliness of Charlotte's example. They would grow old together; and if Charlotte wished the society of men at times, — Jessica thought that a little of it would suffice, — why, Charlotte should be given it.

The patient became convalescent. The case had been less severe than Jessica's fears. Charlotte was able to join with the prayers of the family, and the admonitions of the doctor, in forcing Jessica into the open air. At last Jessica consented to take both exercise and sleep, and while she was absent Charlotte lay musing hour after hour over the girl in the play. It occurred to Jessica to ask the doctor about the rumor of Bond's engagement; the doctor would know. She met the medical man coming from his final visit to Charlotte. Mr. Bond's engagement to Miss Catherwood was a fact which would soon be attested by names engraved. The wedding was to take place in Boston.

Jessica breathed a long sigh of content, and ran up-stairs.

The room was dim in twilight. Charlotte lay motionless, with her hands clasped under her head. She had been long in meditation. There was a settled look upon her face. The heart-crisis was past.

"Jessie dear," she said immediately, "I have something to tell you. I — care for — Mr. Bond."

12

Jessica's heart stopped. She must not speak now — no, not until Charlotte was strong.

"You are not going to be angry, Jessie?" asked Charlotte.

"Oh, no, darling," said Jessica, with a great lump in her throat. She threw her arms around her friend. "You will always need me — no matter what happens!"

"I told you," said Charlotte, pressing her face against Jessica's, "because I am so happy; and I want to tell some one."

"But, my darling," said Jessica, who dared not sob, "you must think only of getting well now. You are not to excite yourself."

"I do not, dearie — I am too happy. It has been so long! I want to be well enough to send for him and ask his pardon. How long will it be?"

"Some time yet, dear. You must think of other things now."

"Think of other things?" said Charlotte, smiling. "You dear, funny girl!"

That evening Jessica read to Charlotte, who listened apparently with close attention; but her thoughts were far away. She was glad to be left alone in the dark when Jessica retired to a night of tears. Charlotte slept and dreamed.

The next day, as Jessica entered the Library, she met Bond.

"Good morning," he said pleasantly, as was his wont to Jessica, notwithstanding her attitude toward him. "Charlotte is ill."

"How did you know?" asked Jessica.

" Because you are alone, if nothing else. I saw the doctor this morning. He gave me your new address, and I sent my wedding-cards to you and Charlotte. Will you step into the florist's? A bunch of violets would look well against that black fur."

She went with him, and this was surprising, for she generally, in his memory of her, took special delight in refusing the smallest courtesy he offered. When he suggested now a huge bunch of violets she declined them. He bowed gravely, and proceeded to assort some roses. Suddenly he said, holding them up :

"I started to pick these out for Miss Catherwood; she likes Banksias, too. But I am going to send them to Charlotte."

" Please don't!" faltered Jessica.

He smiled curiously to himself, and wrote down Charlotte's name and address. When he had added his card to the flowers, Jessica went with him to the street. As they came out she stopped him, and facing him with a pleading such as he never imagined could come to her eyes, she said :

"Won't you please, *please*, not send those flowers to Charlotte?"

He looked at her in amazement.

"Let us cross to the Common," he said.

When they were less in the crowd, he turned to her and said, with wonder, and yet in an indulgent way :

"You are a most extraordinary woman!"

"I will be any kind you wish — if you will only do as I ask," she said almost tearfully.

He marveled to see Jessica humbled to make a prayer to him. It was ridiculous.

" You forget," he said gravely, " that I think a great deal of Charlotte."

" You — think a great deal of her!" said Jessica, impetuously. " Oh, you are no better than all the other clay of your kind! Your sentiments will not stand the wear of two short years. You said you could never love any one but Charlotte — that you would wait for her as long as you lived, that she could summon you in ten years and still find you true. And here you send her your wedding-cards, engraved with another woman's name! What fools women are!"

" It is true that I said all those things," he answered without emotion, " except the last. And many other things which I presume Charlotte held no more sacredly than to tell you — who have so often declared me an impossible person. The answer to your implication that I am a staler of oaths lies in the material you use for your arraignment of me."

" What Charlotte has said to me was in defense of you."

" Silence was all the defense I needed," he said, looking into the distance.

" That is all you have received for two years," said Jessica, mendaciously.

" Then — what more to say? Charlotte is happy, you are happy, I am happy — ah, but that is not all true!" he said sorrowfully. " Charlotte and you are not happy. You have built a wall around yourselves — you have shut yourselves away from sympathy with men, and you are out of the march of life."

" All because neither Charlotte nor I wished her to marry you!" laughed Jessica.

CHARLOTTE gained strength rapidly. She had not lost her hair. This was a source of happiness. She remembered how Bond had often admired it. She amused herself with fondling its full length and thinking of him. Then she blushed in the quiet of her room. Each day brought the spring nearer. Jessica came in every morning laden with flowers, and promising the earliest wild blossoms when they should appear. The twenty-eight white roses Jessica had taken from the box when they came, and they stood on Charlotte's table for three days, apparently as a token of Jessica's affection. Her real tribute was the fact that Bond's card lay in Jessica's room, part of the ashes in the grate. Jessica would not leave the house until the flowers had safely reached her own hands; and until the wedding-cards, too, had come, and were stowed away in her secret drawer. Bond was to be married at noon on the third of May.

By that morning Charlotte had risen and dressed regularly for a week. The weather had been cold and wet, and it was not thought advisable for her to go out. But now the day opened bright and warm. It brought memories of past delightful springtimes and promises of summer that sent her mind back to Seaweed Cove, and to the blue waters over which she had gazed so many hours in silence. Soon she and Jessica would ride out together, and before long Charlotte could consider herself well-nigh restored. For a week Jessica had gone about weighed to earth with the news she felt long overdue to Charlotte. Often it trembled on her lips to speak; but the effort stifled it. When the two were together Jessica's mind was

12*

distracted in debate when and how to begin, while Charlotte's thoughts were too evidently far away.

The crisis came when, on this morning of the third of May, Jessica discovered Charlotte sitting at her desk finishing a note. Charlotte colored crimson when she found Jessica's eyes fixed upon her in a strange, compassionate gaze.

"You are *not* writing to Mr. Bond?"

"Yes, dear. I have asked him to come as soon as he can. The doctor told me he was here — two weeks ago," she confessed shyly. "Oh, it is so delightful to be well again!"

"But how can you be so sure he will come now?" said Jessica.

"Ah — you do not know him! Why should he not, dear?"

"Because, Challie dear — *did n't* the doctor say the rest?" asked Jessica, hopelessly.

"The rest?"

"Yes; that Mr. Bond is going to marry Miss Catherwood? Dearest, I could n't tell you until you were strong."

Charlotte put down her pen. Her color flew. She rested her elbows on the desk and pressed her forehead in her hands. Jessica came and placed her arms around her friend. There was no word.

"I cannot say I am surprised, dear," said Jessica, aimlessly.

There was a long silence in the room. The soft May air came in through the open window. It brought the chiming of the bells in the steeple of the church where Franklin Bond would soon stand before the

altar. It blew the hair which Charlotte had fondled
in thinking of him. For a time she seemed unaware
of Jessica's presence. Suddenly Charlotte rose and
walked across the room.

"I do not believe it," she said resolutely. "I cannot
believe it. Don't you know it was lack of faith that
has made me miserable for two long years? Don't
you know that he never *has* failed to live up to what
I think of him *now?* That was the trouble, Jessica.
When I first knew him I could take no man seriously.
I looked down upon them. What childishness for a
girl of twenty-three! And even when I grew to know
him so well, I could not see that he justified his aspirations. His capital seemed so slim to me then; I
did not recognize the moral part of it. I did not understand that he knew his disadvantages better than
I did, and yet was less afraid in his own self than I
was for him. I saw all his mistakes very clearly; but
I did not see that he never faltered one moment in his
course — he always pressed forward — always; sometimes slowly, sometimes almost standing still; but he
always faced one way, Jessica, and I — I could have
helped him so much more than I did! If I had only
understood! But we laughed at him, and made fun
of his work in the newspapers, and of the little book
which he never published because I did not think it
equal to some masterpiece — and there was no one for
whose opinion he cared as he did for mine. He put
the little book aside; but he never stopped — he went
on just as if I had never existed — only he took more
pride in my praise than — O Jessica! And it made no
difference what idle thing I said, or how I hurt him in

my thoughtless criticisms, or how I showed I thought
him inferior clay — he forgave me; he never lost his
gentle tone for one moment all the time I knew him.
And I thought it was small humility on his part, I
thought it was obeisance to my higher spirit — when
it was only because he knew better and felt more
deeply than I did, and forgave me out of the sweet-
ness of his soul! Oh, we have much to learn! They
teach us to applaud things that are applauded, but we
do not learn to praise the man in the aspiration and
in the struggle. And he never ceased to love me as
long as I — and I do not believe he has ceased to *now!*
If his name has been heard with Miss Catherwood's,
why, it has been against his will. For all I know, perhaps he thought it might move me as it did the girl
in the play. I told you about that. She thought she
had lost him — then she began to feel his value. It
made her wretched first. It made them both happy
in the end. It was a matter of years; but they cared
for each other. Time could not change it. And do
you believe that the man who wrote that sweet little
play, the one who was true to me through three long
years of wretched unappreciation on my part, through
rebuff and insane womanish freaks and distrust and
almost ridicule at times — do you believe he has forgotten the things he said to me? Why, I have faith
now! If you were to tell me anything in the world
against him I would believe him innocent. I have
faith. I believe he loves me to-day — just as he always did. And I — do not deserve it!"

"But, oh, my darling!" cried Jessica, bursting into
tears, "he does n't love you any more! He told me
so — and I have been the cause of all this!"

"I have faith in him!" said Charlotte. "He would not open his heart to you."

"But he is being married away at this minute — in the church under those bells. I have his cards, addressed to you. *Must* you see?"

"Let me have them!" gasped Charlotte.

Charlotte stood at the window, holding to the sill in the whirl of things about her. The current of spring air struck cold against her heated temples. Her note to Bond rustled and blew from the table. The church lay in the distance before her. The chimes rang out the wedding-march from "Lohengrin," and the people would soon begin to stream from the portal. Her breath came quick and irregular. She thrust her arms out wide above her head, and appealed to the fresh blue sky with a sigh that shook her frame. Jessica returned wet-eyed, with the invitation in her hand. Charlotte was rigid. She took the smooth paper in her hands — the lines swam — she did not see the names. Jessica dropped to her knees, and beseechingly clasped Charlotte, crying:

"Can you ever in the long, long world forgive me?"

The paper floated to the floor. Charlotte's hands fell lightly on Jessica's shoulders. The silence was broken only by Jessica's sobs.

"There is nothing to forgive," said Charlotte at length, slowly. "I was put to a test. I was offered doubt and mistrust — and I accepted them. I was unequal to the test. Mr. Bond has to thank you. There is nothing."

"Say that we can go on now," pleaded Jessica, tearfully — "go on as we did before ever a man came into our happiness. I will give my whole life to

make you forget—my whole life! Poor, poor darling
Charlotte!"

Charlotte slowly shook her head:

"It can never be exactly the same—not until we
understand each other. I do not want to forget. It
is not I who am to be pitied. I am better off than
you. I have learned. I would not for anything in the
world exchange my—for the man who once—for
your innocence of what it is to trust—!"

THAT was two years ago. Charlotte is thirty. I
do not know that she is prominent in charitable work,
or has thrown herself into some intellectual field with
an energy and devotion that are winning her laurels.
I have not heard that she is specially glorified as the
sweet fireside aunt of her brother's children, or the
tender confidante of younger people in love. But I
know that her hair has in it many threads of purest
silver; and that she looks quite thirty; and that—I
should not like to be Charlotte.

Jessica was married last fall to a man four years
younger than herself.

ENTER THE EARL OF TYNE

S Mr. Howard Delafield turned from Seventy-blank street into the avenue, a sleigh with scarlet plumes and a crystal dasher rushed past him and drew up in front of the Garston house. The Earl of Tyne alighted, and the footman had hardly touched the bell before the door opened and the earl went in. Mr. Delafield, on foot, paused for an instant in the middle of a step, and then kept on past the Garston house, as if that had not been his destination. He decided to return in half an hour, and, if the sleigh was gone, ring the bell — to find, probably, that Mildred had left for a ride with the earl and her grandmother. If so, Mr. Delafield would have to explain his late delinquencies on another day. It seemed a month since he had seen Mildred; but he was not quite loath to delay what now he knew he should say. He had been heavy-hearted all the way, and the rich spectacle of the earl and of the glistening sleigh and its men and jingling steeds made Delafield sick.

But when he came back the sleigh was gone. Miss Garston had not ridden off with the earl. She was in; and she greeted Delafield coolly, and led the way to the oak room, where a log fire crackled on the hearth.

"I don't understand," she began, turning in the fuller light; but her tone altered a shade. "Are you ill? Could n't you come?"

"I 'm all right," he said, with a weary smile, taking the arm-chair. "It 's a long story; I ought to have written."

"I don't see why you did n't write," she said. "It has been a week. I could n't ask any one; I simply lay awake. There 's so little defense of ignoring me. It 's against all our theories, and I never should hesitate to withdraw rather than accept it. I don't want to be hasty. You look pale, and I 'm sorry; but you make me suffer, and you don't seem to understand, and you might as well be in Japan."

"I never should withhold my confidence," said Delafield. "I could n't respect you if I did. So we shall not part for that. It is good," he added ominously, "that we can be calm over serious things."

"But what is so serious?" she asked, frightened from some of her color. "Tell me, have I seemed to do something? Surely you don't believe that about the earl — that I let him pay me marked attention? I wondered if those reporters had talked to you and added to the falsehoods they printed about him. I tried to fit a dozen reasons to your silence, but I could n't fit one. I saw you hurrying along Twenty-third street two days ago, and you did n't look disabled. Don't you see how queer — "

"Do you know how long we have been engaged?" he asked gravely.

"Nearly three years," said Mildred, as if the time had not seemed long.

"And you are twenty-four years old, and I am as impecunious as I was three years ago. We can't go on this way — we must give it up."

He did not look to see her face, but gazed intently on the flames.

"I thought then," he said, after a few moments, "that by now we might be married. I really had done well when I reached the editorial staff, and I thought I should soon have something better. But I did n't. Beyond a few hundreds saved, I have n't since made a gain. I 've gone off; my chances have decreased; and I don't seem doomed to financial success. But in my capacity of one who treasures your welfare I will not be a fiasco. We must give it up, and you must take what better fate awaits you."

She was rigid in the oak settee, with her eyes fixed on the Garston arms below the mantel. He shook his head in pity of himself.

"I 've had time," he went on, in a strained voice, "to think. A man may be much that a woman honors, and yet from a metropolitan point be a financial failure. We both thought the chances favorable; but they are not. In four or five years I might, by dint of plodding, take you to Harlem, but not the best of it, to share my nonentity in 'apartments' — a set of bins a hundred feet in the sky — a euphemism for a tenement. I could not promise more. You would be excommunicated from society because you could not afford to entertain, and debarred from the opera because you would not climb the heavens to hear it. Then you would find, after the novelty of our life had settled to a routine, that you were slowly dying of distaste, and that the only happy ones about you were those who could be content with farce-comedy and popular music and Sunday newspapers."

The Garston arms were silver set in purple marble, and her face was cold against them. Her feet were motionless on the tiger's skin. Delafield appeared to be making a painful study of the flames. He started on, and had to begin twice.

"Food, clothing, warmth, friends," he said, clearing his throat — "all are necessary. They cost in New York. You must have finery if you move with the friends of the Earl of Tyne; you must have things to feed to them, and a place to receive them in. We must n't learn by dire experience what is so patent; if there is an art of living, we ought to consider the end, and allow for our older years, with your greater needs for dainties and carriages and servants and climates. It is inevitable that some day you would compare your state with what it might have been, and me — with the other man; and I am not sure I should be adequate; I cannot advise the risk. The woman who marries a fortune is something assuaged if her love wears out; and for you no brilliant marriage is improbable. I should never forget that, left to your present surroundings, you might have come to care for a man of great wealth, or perhaps for one with both wealth and title, like the Earl of Tyne. And, on the other hand, to see you condemned with me to such a contrast with what might have been, would destroy the lightness of my heart."

The fire was subsiding. He paused. Very far away she seemed already, with her eyes, half closed, fixed

on the gaping lion's mouth in the arms. He could not
read her face. She might be occupied with some
scornful misinterpretation.

"I would n't have you think that I despair," he said
suddenly. "I always go on. My philosophy does not
refuse me self-esteem; and it could n't refuse success,
if life were forever and strength as long as life. But
a woman ages; she cannot so well begin a career in
the middle of her prime. If you wait and wait, and
curb all thoughts of other men, and finally *do* see me
crushed — think of it! See how it stands now. I am
no longer an editorial writer — I have not been for a
week. I have changed my rooms, so that the book
reviews can meet my present expense. I shall find
something else, simply because a man can't seek in
vain forever. I left because they asked me to libel
Dougherty, our misrepresentative in Congress, and to
twist his foolish doings to the semblance of a misde-
meanor. Dougherty does n't know enough to be a
rascal; and I refused, and they gave me a choice, and
I resigned. Affairs have promised this for months;
for my self-respect grew always faster than my bank-
account, and some of the things I used to condone are
abhorrent to me now. I cannot call a college graduate
a noble fellow because he ferrets out a girl who fled
away to hide, and because he purchases her photo-
graph from the villain who swore to defend her. But
that is what first promoted my successor. For a long
time I have refused to write some things they asked,
and they found me worth concessions, though they
knew how strongly I stood for reform ideas and how
contemptible I held their party majors; but the new

13

man can do perhaps as well as I, and he stops at
nothing.   He is an example of "perfect discipline";
he knows the division between moral and legal libel
to a hair's breadth.   I used to dream how satisfactory
it must be to be a gentleman of the editorial column
and wield nothing but a force toward better things.
I thought then, you see, that all journalism was a professional pursuit.   If I had been less callow it would
have been far better for you."

Her fingers lay on the arm of the settee, and the
diamond on one of them — the only jewel she wore —
shot up a cold glint caught and changed from the lessening rays of the fire.   He could see only her profile.

"There is one thing I never have spoken of," he
said, after a moment, compressing his lips.   "I should
be absurd to ignore that your grandmother is a rich
woman who loves you and likes me well.   In the event
of her death you would receive a fortune by her will,
or she might give you an income if you married.
Both these possibilities may have crossed your mind
as fair guaranties for the future; but have you reflected how the prospect of being the impecunious
husband of a rich wife would load me with dread?
My pride would not bear it — nor yours — for me to
be a weakling beside your beauty and your money.
It has not frightened me away, you understand; it
has made me pause, for your sake.   It has brought me
to a determination which nothing can alter."

Her pallor was disturbing him.   She was like ala-
baster, and the rise of her chest was barely apparent.
She had not spoken, or moved her eyes from the Garston arms.   The blaze had left the hearth, and the

logs smoldered, growing blacker and blacker, while
the sky outside took deeper and colder tints, and the
winter sun was sinking in a flare of orange. He feared
that she mistrusted his sincerity.

"I may have seemed unimpassioned all through our
engagement," he said, with regretful firmness. "But
if I have seemed so, you will thank me. I know I
hurt you. I shall not speak of myself — it is not the
time; but I submit that, if you release me, it will be
better for us to — say good-by — now. Only your
grandmother knows that we have been engaged; and
we have always maintained a dignity which you will
not regret, perhaps, when we meet again in after years.
That is all. Am I not right?"

He had finished. What he had doubted his courage
for when he had sighted Mildred's house, the Earl of
Tyne had given him strength to say. Now the words
were out of his mouth, and as he waited for Mildred's
answer his mind went back to the room in West
Twenty-eighth street where he was going after he had
parted with Mildred for perhaps the rest of their lives.
It was a dingy and darksome and narrow room, no
whit less melancholy for the presence of his bookcase
and his desk and his books and etchings. It was a
wretched place to go and lie awake in the first appall-
ing realization of his sacrifice; it was wretched because there on the table, in a silver frame with doors
that were unlocked by a sacred key, would be the picture of Mildred — Mildred as he had seen her once on
the stairs, on the night of a ball. The frame had stood
on his table for two long years, to be opened as often
as he paused at early morning, after his work was

done, before he went to dream of her. Whatever he did, the picture, or the absence of it, would dominate the room, and the room would dominate him. He would give up the room, he told himself; he would take his savings and wander abroad until the wound stopped bleeding. But even then he could never again unlock the silver frame, nor — unless he heard some day that Mildred was a countess — ever part with it.

Mildred was still mute and white. The maid came knocking, and opened the portières to fetch some wood.

"It's gun out, ma'am," she said, from her knees, as she placed a small log on the andirons and poked the embers into a heap beneath. "Should I start it or leave it?"

"Yes," murmured Mildred, with unwitting ambiguity; and the maid, aware of an oblivion chilling even to a servant, forsook the fire to its will. Delafield turned to Mildred and paused for her answer. She began to breathe harder, and seemed about to speak; but she could not. He asked himself wretchedly how one could doubt her who saw her eyes so blank with woe, and saw the clasping and unclasping of her fingers. Her mouth twitched as if she was a tiny girl and as if he had been treacherous and made her afraid of every one. In an escape of tenderness he let himself for a moment cover her hand.

"Why, you poor child," he exclaimed, "it's as cold as ice! What makes it so?"

"It's the ring," she said huskily, her eyes shunning him. "I — I release you!"

She took the diamond off and laid it on the arm of the settee.

"But — please keep it," he said, at the memory of how he had put it on her finger many months ago. "You 'll keep at least that, won't you?"

"You forget it was your mother's — that she told you to give it to the woman you loved" said Mildred, with a trace of bitterness. "Only," she added, turning to him, "just for a while will you sit here? I want to say some things, if I can, that would have come to me when you were gone — things I should suffer not to say. Once I could n't have asked you; but three years make a change. I cannot readjust myself so quickly — with no warning. Will you come?" she asked faintly.

He moved to the place beside her on the double settee. The fire, lingering along the bottom of the logs, reflected some glow from the hearth, brighter because the twilight was beginning. The white diamond glittered on the settee arm, minus an owner. Mildred kept half turned away from him, and he waited for her to go on.

"It 's because ours has been so — different from others," she said, struggling for words. "Other men are much more — more enthusiastic to the women who promise to marry them. But you seem to have thought you ought n't to be, or else you did n't care. And I always feared to say — perhaps — how good you were."

She paused for a moment.

"Because," she went on, "I could n't — in words — they mock me, and you left no other way. If you

13*

had n't been outwardly so true and careful, and so
fierce in your hatred of fraud, I should have thought
you could n't have much feeling. But, as it was, I
believed you meant to honor me."

Delafield was looking into the embers.

" You 've been so different from what I expected —
when you asked me. You were *so* good then! I had
read your heart from the instant you came to care. I
knew for weeks that you were weighing it over; and
I was *so* proud of you for first telling me about — your
prospects. Perhaps you thought I did n't appreciate
that; and I 'm sure you were shocked at my quick
assent, for you did n't know how I had wished it for
months and months. And now you think that what
I accepted so readily I can easily lose. You never will
know; for I am not as I was. I used to quench my
doubts, but I can't be certain now whether you ever
cared or not."

The embers were fading out, and her face was re-
ceding in the gloom.

" How little I know you," she went on, the words
coming faster, " that I can talk so — after these years!
It 's because you placed me too high, perhaps; made
me a goddess instead of a friend. I did n't want to
be a goddess; it is n't a real thing. I wanted to be
like other well-bred women when they give their word.
But I could n't ask you to be different; I could n't
speak of it now if I ever expected to see you again.
My friendship did n't attract you. You saw this house
and the precious girdles I wear, and you concluded
that I was too dainty to be useful, and too feeble to
stand the battle of life — for any sake; and you liked

me because I made a pretty ornament in this background, just as you part with me because you cannot maintain it. I was foolish not to see that. You enjoy in me the very contrast with what I admired in you. You have never seen any one just like me; and when you found me in such surroundings, not pampered or silly or spoiled, I impressed you. It must have been because I looked well standing at the head of the stairs, with the stained-glass light, and the maid lifting on my cloak, and the footman waiting stiff below with my traveling-bag — as you saw me once, and looked so worshipful. How strange you were not to know that you were stronger and better and finer a sight than I! At that moment I should have rather gone with you, with a cheap bag and a cheap cloak and no footman and no maid, than have gone as I did, with any one else in the world. I did n't know you then as I do to-day. The maid and the stained glass had been traditions in our family simply because wealth and elegance had been traditions; but *they* did n't make our happiness. Health was what we asked, and the joy of exerting strength and will, whether it was my grandfather in his ship or my father in his bank. If you think I have degenerated from them, you are neither clever nor complimentary."

The darkness had pressed down between them, though she sat so near. The solitary diamond sparkled close to her fingers' ends. He heaved a deep, uneven sigh; but Mildred's voice was growing stronger.

"I should have seen how far apart our real ideals lay; but I was foolish, and I do thank you for your dignity now. You differed so from the men I was

meeting.   They were either stupid or gross, or jellied
with vice, or poor cartoons of foreigners.   There was
n't one of them with the grace of the Earl of Tyne,
and there was n't one of them like our people — like
my father.   But you were so ambitious and vigorous
and daring!   You had even done brutal things, I
thought, though I admired the dash that took you
through them, because I felt that better taste would
come to you, as it has.   In most things you had all
the finish of the men I knew, and you realized twice
as much as they dreamed.   You had struggled, too,
and suffered anxiety and temptation; and yet you
were as ruddy and clear-skinned and steady-handed
as a young girl.   You grew — I could see you grow;
and you called to all that was potent and healthy in
my mind.   I wanted to run beside you, and do and
dare things with you, and live your life of vigor and
conquest.   I did n't want to be carried — I 'm too much
alive.   I knew I could not run so fast or so far as you;
but I could go each day faster and farther than you
could carry me.   I used to tell you this, and you used
to say what a mighty team two such as we would be
when we both put shoulder to the wheel, each to his
best.   But you did n't mean it, or else you meant it
for all the world but me.   Your real picture was a girl
at the head of the stairs, waiting freshly groomed and
gowned, all crisp and idle and full of pretty feminine affairs to dissipate your weariness and vexations.
That has its fascination, true enough, and quite enough,
for most of us; but it is n't the thing for me.   I 'm
too jealous of your hours away from me — I mean I
should be if I cared.   I should expect your life-work

to be part of your soul, and I should want to be part
of it in some way, too. I should want to serve wherever I could, being your friend — the best you ever
had. I should lose the last memory of myself in the
one I cared for. That would be living — for me. But
you — would n't understand it."

A screen stopped most of the light that would have
come in through the windows, and the fire was hidden
in its own ashes. They were in the dark. The chim-
ney-place was growing cold; the sleigh-bells in the
street, recalling the Earl of Tyne, sounded cold, too;
and the cruel things she said were tingling. He had
not thought that words would ever hurt him from so
sweet a source.

"Then if you failed," she continued, "I should know
it was fate, not lack of me; just as a triumph would
n't be yours alone, but ours, as life would be ours. A
woman who asks that, who can let you go without a
pang because you fail to value it — she would never
be a drag, no matter how much she had to learn. I
have no genius, I know; I can't write; and so you
think my energies would be dispersed by society —
that I should languish for the Earl of Tyne! You
have n't believed me when I said I had no taste for
that. I 'm not opposed to social life; I know it too
well: it keeps more people out of mischief than it
spoils. But it is n't the thing for me. I have vigor
that will not let me dawdle; and independence and
will that never betrayed me until I thought I cared
for you. I don't wonder you mistake me; I never
am so timid and weak as with you; nor so stupid as
not to see when I 'm made a sport of."

She stopped for a moment.

"But you wrong me, Mildred!" he said painfully.

"I never wronged you while I expected to be your wife," came her spirited answer. "I took in earnest everything you said. Life means so much to me; it has so many charms — such great rewards for force and action; its very buffets have a taste for me. You never imagined for an instant what terrific impatience I leashed from day to day since we were first engaged; how I longed to grasp your hand and be off and be living. You would have thought it bold if I had told you while we were engaged. Oh, I used some days to walk in Central Park all the morning; to tire myself and keep myself from lying awake to think how I might help you. If I did n't, I wanted to fly — to jump from my window. What a waste it was — a waste of thought and sleepless nights, when I could rise in the morning and walk my miles and yet come back sleepless, because I longed to be up and working out the traditions of my blood! And all my dreams pointed to you, who took me for nothing — nothing but lace! You don't know me. You don't know what I like, or what I need, or how little you fulfill your promise. You think I want carriages! I 'd rather have a driving snow and high boots and an alpenstock, with a loaf of rye bread in a haversack, than tool a coach with the Earl of Tyne through ten columns of a newspaper. You think I should languish in a flat with a man who was mine and knew me through and through — languish for want of a box at the Metropolitan, and for want of an earl when I had my own nobleman plighted to me gladly! You apprehend me, but you cannot comprehend me in the least."

The soft fabric of her sleeve touched his shoulder; but he felt as far removed from her as if three years ago she had not laid her head upon his shoulder and said she was happy there. Delafield winced.

"But you don't know the dreary reality," he said hopelessly. "You never knew rude living except as a bit of contrast. You have n't felt its deadening power."

"You could n't deaden me with rude living if I chose to accept it," she exclaimed angrily. "You could n't break my spirit with plain walls so long as there was air and sky and the elements of food. I know it deadens the dead; it frets small souls; it would stimulate me. If it would n't, there is no such thing as binding hearts. If a strong woman cannot share your lot as honor makes it, then she never loved you more than half. If you don't expect that principle, you don't honor her and you don't care. I know my words are only sounds to you; I ought to say, 'I adore you — if you can furnish steam heat and all the modern improvements!' You 'd respect me just as much if I did. But now you think I 'm melodramatic, and I think you are; for every word you spoke has been affected. If we had gone on as we did until we married, our misunderstanding would have finished, but our mistake would have only begun. You are not keyed up to my pitch," she said passionately. "You 've taken three good years of my life under false pretenses; and you 've humiliated me so that I 'm ashamed to look at you, and I 'm glad it 's dark!"

"Ah, but you *don't* know!" he protested wretchedly, gripping the back of the settee so that it creaked. "And you don't know how hard it has been to say it! I should have been a coward and held it back if I had n't seen him coming up your steps. I had started in indecision, and every step saw me worse; but his splendor made me sick. If you care no more than you say, I 'm already — but you must care, Mildred; you would n't speak so hotly if you did n't."

"Then I 'll speak more calmly," she said, with what seemed self-possession. "We both have much to thank the earl for, it seems. Has the fire quite gone out? Perhaps you find it chilly here?" she added, turning to him in the gloom.

He made no answer, but his hand dropped from the back of the settee.

"I 'll go now," he said at last, trying to adopt her manner. Yet he waited, while she kept silent, and heard his breathing, and saw the sparkle of his diamond just beyond her finger-tips. A cold draft blew down through the chimney and swept the ashes.

"There 'll be a time," he said, "when you 'll look upon me as only a newspaper man, without distinction from all the rest. *He* will see me, and he 'll think of the vulgar, venal irresponsibility of the most blatant of our newspapers, of the sort that traduce their ignorant readers and affront their intelligent ones with every revolution of their press; and he 'll say contemptuously, 'That is one of the men who write what they would blush to own.' And yet there are clean sheets, for those who have taste for them; and one may be both a journalist and a gentleman; and if not, he 'd only be one in ignominy with the thousands who bought what he wrote. But when a few years are gone all I shall be to you is — a newspaper man."

"If a man respects himself, that should be enough," she said coldly, as if she did not divine that he was thinking of the earl.

Delafield stood up. He paused for a moment, and she knew he was trying to discern for the last time her outline in the darkness. Then slowly he made his way around back of the settee, past tables and chairs, to the door. She heard the clink of the rings of the portières, and could tell that he had paused again, holding the curtain in his hand. She realized that the next few moments would shape the course of her life.

"Oh, will you please find the bellows for me before you go?" she asked in a new tone suited to pleading for a favor.

He came groping his way back, with hands outstretched, and accidentally touched her face. She gave a little start and an exclamation which he did not comprehend. The maid turned the current on in the hall, and some light came over the top of the portières.

"Did I hurt you?" he asked. "I could n't see."

"No — I understand," she hastened to say, with a shiver. She had thought he meant a caress. "I wanted the bellows to blow the fire, please. I'm cold."

He picked it out, and, as he would have done when they had been engaged, used it on the ashes to save her the trouble of it. At first the embers took some life; then they drowsed.

"It's gone too far," he said grimly; "it won't come up again."

"Oh, I *think* it will," she said fervently, "if you only try!"

He kept on mechanically, looking into the embers; but they gave no more than a glow that seemed to compensate for the pallor of his face.

"It's no use," he said at length, letting the mouth of the bellows drop, and staring dejectedly into the ashes.

"Don't be disgusted," she urged, so softly as if she feared to frighten the flames away. "Can't you try again?"

"I'll send the maid; I'll ring the bell as I go out," he said, keeping turned away from her, and about to rise.

"But you're not going to force me to make the fire myself?" she asked gently, laying her hand on his sleeve and looking earnestly at him. "I don't want the maid. I want you — you to move the log a trifle, please — to where those splinters will catch. I'm too cold to wait for the maid, and I want to say one little word more. Please take the stool."

He did as she asked, and with the tongs moved the log to where the splinters took the flames; and as she watched him, silently and with hungry eyes, the fire ran along until all the log was ablaze and crackling and lighting the room. He waited, not seeing her face, and growing bitter that she should be able to add to the injuries she had already inflicted.

"About the earl," she began, with difficulty — "I have seen him only three times in my life. We were introduced at Mrs. Van Thaler's, and we talked for

about ten minutes. I did not go to ride with him, as
the papers said; and I never showed that I liked him.
Last week he called here, and I was astonished and
grandma was enraged; but we saw that he was under
some delusion. To-day, just as I sent a servant to
buy your paper to see if it chanced to mention your
whereabouts, he came again. We had never asked
him to come to see us. In a little while I managed
to find what his mistake was. He took me for Miss
Gaston, farther up the avenue; he did n't know that
our name was Garston. He said she had invited him,
but that he had forgotten her face and remembered
only her name, which was known all over the world
in connection with a great business house; and he
said he had forgotten my name, but remembered my
face. I told him that we knew the Gastons but
slightly. Then he apologized very regretfully, and
went away. I don't know him."

She waited wistfully for Delafield to make some
comment, but he did not.

"And grandma could n't leave me anything," she
said, miserable at his silence. "It all goes to charity,
because papa was wealthy then, and grandpa did n't
expect him to die so poor, and so they arranged it all
between them. I shall have just my own little income.
I wear these things only because grandma insists on
buying them; but when she 's gone I shall have only
my few hundreds, and *they* ought n't to be enough to
frighten even you away."

She paused and waited in vain. Delafield said
nothing. Her eyes fell on the diamond, and its
sparkle was too much for them.

"I did n't have any *more* to say," she faltered, half choking. "I — I thought —"

The tears that had assembled behind her vehemence rushed up in triumph over her striving, and she trembled and shuddered with her grief. For a moment Delafield clenched his fists behind him; then they opened, and he moved quickly to her side.

"Shall I love my happiness more than you?" he said distinctly. "Shall I follow my heart alone?"

"Yes — yes; be selfish — be selfish!" cried Mildred. "I — I want to be worth fury and hate and fighting for! There is n't anything in the world I want so much as you!"

He took her strongly in his arms, and tenderly kissed her. She was still sobbing, but differently; and he let her weep for the easing of her heart.

"I shall adopt your view," he said resolutely, with his lips at her ear. "From now I shall believe all you believe; and we 'll start and make our life a proof of our creed. Don't fear that I shall be weak; I was thinking of you, and I made a mistake. I always go on. Please —"

"Yes," she said joyously, her arms around his neck and their eyes meeting in new trust and happiness; "you were tired and worn with anxiety, and the earl bothered you, dear. But it will not be so again, because first you 'll tell me everything. You must take a long rest to-night; but you must stay to dinner, and drink something hot to prevent you from having gotten cold while I was *so* horrid."

With her repentance she was nearly ready to weep again, and she sprang up on a plea of drawing the shades. There came a heavy clang of sleigh-bells without, different from the ordinary.

"Come quick!" she said.

She had looked out in the glare of the electric lights and had seen the sleigh with the scarlet plumes and the crystal dasher. There were the two splendid towering flunkies, strictly *en profil;* and behind them, half frozen in their furs, the young Earl of Tyne, elegantly dressed, and a brilliantly costumed girl of countenance sharp and sagacious.

Delafield came up behind Mildred and slipped the diamond to its place on her lovely finger.

"And who 's the lady?" he asked.

"That 's Miss Gaston," said Mildred.

THE SPIRIT IN THE PIPE

ELL, I 'll tell ye. Captain Silas Farragut Tarrant, U. S. N., owned a farm whereon was a barn wherein was a horse over which was a room where slept a little red Irishman — Clarence O'Shay — who loved both the pipe and the jug. Which I say no word agin um, but one night the rum rose up in O'Shay and the coals dropped out of uz pipe aflame on the straw of uz bed, and the barn burnt down and the horse burnt up.

And Clarence O'Shay ran that fast away from the blaze that when the Captain had um up on charge of cruelty to a beast and arsony to a barn, Clarence come into court with an alibi; whereby the jury acquit um of arsony, by that he could n't have possibly been at the barn at the time; and fined um twenty dollars for cruelty to a beast because at such time he ought to have been at the barn.

And the Captain, as some say, to make amends for the charge found false, or as others say to git O'Shay before an impudent cocked-hat court some day, instid of a civil one, got an enlistment for O'Shay as a second-class blue-jacket in the navy, and then straightway forgot of um. For the Captain was busy with

trading of uz hot-skotched farm and with having uz
rich wife's relations tickle the administration to git
um a fine command.

And they fixed it to shove aside the one that should
have ut and give old Tarrant command of the battle-
ship *Utah*, U. S. N., a brand-new grand machine of
war of thirteen thousand ton by specification and
fourteen thousand by fact, they say; she had a
whole grove of funnels and military tops and wicked
rifles pointing every what way. And the Captain come
aboard of her and hoisted his pennant and declared
she was in commission. But 't was three months before he had her ready to commit anything but lying
forninst the pier.

Well, Clarence O'Shay, going his way, was sent to
a big fat wooden receiving-ship — one of the war of
1812. That 's where I see um first; a square, short,
squat, raw squab he was, with brick-colored fur and
a jaw like the end of a box; and uz shanks was twisted
like andirons' legs. There was two or three hundred
aboard, some recruits like him, and some with their
hides tanned with experience, like me. I made a friend
of um because he said that old Tarrant was beholden
to um.

And the officers took um and put um through the
setting-up exercises day by day, till uz shoulder blades
ground the skin of uz back between um and the beads
stood out on uz brow, and they had um straightened;
and they swore at um till they filled um with respect;
and they taught um the evil end of a gun, and a notion of standing in line and counting fours and drill-
ing with the rest of the tarriers; and I learned um

how to swing to uz hammick without kicking all four
of uz neighbors out of bed; and he got the gift of ut
in three months, and no credit to uz stupidity.

And when we made part of a draft of fifty to fill
out the *Utah* I took um under me wing and showed
um how to smuggle uz jug in the broad light of day
past the searching sergeant of marines; and he took
to that handily. But — oh, a real man-o'-war was a
wildering bedazzlement to um! 'T was cross-eyeing
to um! Such that he spent the deal of uz time a-fall-
ing through coal-holes and hatches and ladderways,
all by mistake — that green he was — and making
friends everywhere in the bowels of the ship by ut,
with telling how once he had risked uz life to save
the Captain's horse from being dry-smoked. And I
thought I see me way to some special dispensations
from old Tarrant through O'Shay.

And I took um a walk — to rub off uz luster. I
showed um the air-pumps and steam-pumps and hand-
pumps and hydraulicky-pumps, and the fan-gear and
tiller-gear and turning-gear; and condinsers and ice-
makers and forty small engines here and there; with
the winches and capstans and dynamos, and ash-hoists
and shot-lifts and railways, and deck-plates and hand-
wheels, and water-tight doors and holds and bottoms
— me telling um what each and every one was for.
And I expostulated to um how the green-flanged red-
painted pipe overhead carried water, and the yellow-
flanged blue pipe carried steam from the donkey, and
the black-flanged gray pipe carried pressed air, and
the red-flanged green pipe carried hydraulicky, and
the speaking-tube pipe, painted yellow, took whispers

all over the ship; and I showed um twenty flush
hatches and started to tell um what each one was for.
But O'Shay took to drink — saying that Heaven would
forgive um.

And he nursed uz jug till he emptied it — and that
with all stragglers aboard and us lying in the lower
harbor with every one sobering for a cruise! And he
laid down on the tank-tops and sing:

> I 'd rather be right than Prisident!
> I 'd rather be boggled than right, bedad!
> *Pop !* — goes the goozle!

and such profanity. And when I asked um to brace
up uz back and temper uz voice to the regulations he
said he was too busy with uz joy. And I begged
um and begged um for fear of court-martial and
me losing uz influence to straighten umself — but
in vain; and when I spilled a bucket of brine on uz
head he said he was tight — tight — water-tight; and
he asked if I was a blue bag-pipe with red fringes —
that obvious to uz surroundings he was; and when I
give um me boot in uz ribs he laughed with joy and
said 't was the pleasantest sensation in the history of
man.

And so for fear of uz court-martial for smuggling
uz jug I lifted a man-hole door and doubled um up
and stuffed um down between the inner and outer
skins of the ship — 't was a space not three feet in the
clear; and I closed um in with a light to sleep by and
screwed down the nuts on the door hard and fast.

And the last command I heard him say was to lower no more blasted coffins there, but to leave um in the gentlemanly enjoyment of uz tomb.

Well, I hauled off and forgot of um. For I see by the signs that the ship was to crawl away by moonlight, and me to serve me lick at the wheel at midnight. So I hove to and snored in me hammick between me favorite beams. And there was little Clarence, forty feet below, lying boxed up on the hard cement of her outside bottom, with her inner bottom for uz sky — not two feet above uz nose, and uz feet agin her vertical keel and uz head bang up agin another vertical plate called a longitudinal. For ye see, a steel man-o'-war's shell is built on the cellulose system, — as though ye should cut off one story of an empty honey-comb and bend ut to the shape of a ship's bottom; and this was one of the cells which six of 'em made a compartment on the *Utah*. And ye could crawl from one of the six to another by virtue of holes in the upright plates; but beyond the six of the compartment ye could n't go without tearing through a twelve-pound plate, unless by the man-hole door, which was screwed down tight above Clarence's head.

But O'Shay laid absorbing the flavor of uz drink long past when old Tarrant come aboard from a champagne goozle, two-thirds content with the universe and placing main reliance on uz executive officer. The Captain ordered the *Utah* under way and tumbled into uz bunk; and I heard the anchor hauling utself in over the windlass and the engines begin

to go bump — bump, bump — bump, and I knew in
me sleep we was off hunting for bad weather for a
sea-test.

And by and by, down below, O'Shay half waked
in uz sleep and inquired the time of day, and no one
answered um — nothing but the stamping of the old
double-harnessed elephants of engines two hundred
feet abaft of um. And he laid on uz back with the electric handlight at uz side gazing up at the black man-
hole door, and by inches he partly come to himself —
seeing above um and below um and all around um
nothing but cold red iron walls and hearing the hard
pounding of something not very far off, he did n't
know what.   And then a cold shiver chased utself all
over um, for the thought of uz being buried alive in
an iron casket that way. " Begad," he says, " I remember now I died with only a boot in the ribs for
me absolution," he says, " and begad I hear the tread
of the twelve apostles plain as day ! "   And with that
he drew in a breath like a wheezy cylinder and let out
a howl to 'em for a stay of proceedings on uz soul ; but
he might as well have been a rat a-drownding in the
bilge ; for the twelve apostles kept on treading, treading,— bump, bump,— never no farther and never no
nearer — keeping step all the time as if they was
walking in a circle round um enjoying the fun of ut.
And he give a shriek and tried to jump up, but the
iron skin struck uz head and knocked um down, and
he saw a hole that let into the next cell and he crawled
through ut like a wild snake, dragging the light and
leaving uz wits and pieces of uz breeches behind um,
first praying and begging of the apostles, and then a-

swearing at 'em and then a-cursing of the Captain's
horse for burning up and leaving um to be buried alive
at sea, and all the time crawling and howling and cold-
sweating till he crawled through the six cells back
again to the first; — and he laid down on uz face and
weep with distaste of ut.

When uz tears was spent he found that uz hand
was grasping of a pipe. And seeing ut was painted
yellow O'Shay come to umself a bit, and remembered
what 't was, for sure. For ye see, the speaking-tube
pipes in the *Utah* was led down through the inner
bottom to keep 'em safe from splinters and shell; and
this happened to be the one that went forward from
the Captain's bunk — the same I showed um in the
pilot-house, with telling um if he was captain he could
speak with me through ut. And O'Shay took out his
grandfather's knife, with the file in ut, and sawed
away at the brass pipe to make a hole in ut; and he
recollected the flask in uz pocket and took comfort by
that; and he filed like a good one, and emptied the
flask, and soon he had a hole in the pipe as big as a
dollar; and he put his big mouth to ut and says:
"Phe-euw!" with a breath that blowed the brass fil-
ings a jingling for yards abaft. And the automatic
mouth-piece aft in the Captain's cabin — 't was nigh
on to midnight — and the same like mouth-piece forrard in the pilot-house, both whistled to wake the
dead. For ye see, Clarence being in the middle, was
establishing umself with both ends of ut — though he
had no thoughts but of me. And the quartermaster's
mate in the pilot-house jumped to the mouth-piece
and whispered: "Yessir." And in the cabin old Tar-

rant, waked up from uz champagne doze by the hiss in uz ear, took up the mouth-piece that hung by a flexible tube from the sheathing, and says with impatience: "Well, sir?" Which neither of 'em heard the other; but O'Shay, down below, hearing their voices associating together, shouts: "Come and unlock me, ye blasted idiot!" And the quartermaster's mate, thinking old Tarrant was locked in his stateroom, says: "Yessir!" and charged horse and foot along the deck toward the cabins. And old Tarrant, at hearing such marvelous insubordination shouted to um by some one at the other end of the tube, shot up from uz bunk like a mortar. "Ye 're under arrest!" says he, through the mouth-piece. "Go tell the master-at-arms to lock ye up!" says he. And O'Shay, thinking ut was me, shook uz fist at the hole in the pipe, and bawls in old Tarrant's ear: "Under arrest, is ut? I 'm ten miles under dry land!" says he. "Come lemme out — or I 'll make a corpse of ye that can't walk the streets of Heaven in decency!" and with hearing that blasphemy the Captain leapt over and pushed a bell, and uz Scandinavian blockhead of a private-of-marines-orderly come in. "Arrest that man in the pilot-house, ye numbskull!" orders the Captain.

And the private-orderly-numbskull lit out for the pilot-house, running to split uz tight blue robin's-egg breeches; and he meets the quartermaster's mate running and asking: "What 's the matter with the skipper?"— and says the orderly: "What 's the matter at the pilot-house?" and they both went on without answering each other. And the mate burst into the

Captain's stateroom, saying eagerly: "Did ye want help, sir?" "Help, ye fool!" roars the Captain. "Who said ut? Do I want help to put on me trousers? You 're under arrest, too, sir! Go tell the orderly to arrest ye despite yer resistance!" he says, or something like ut. "I'll see if there's mutiny aboard this craft," says old Tarrant, putting his feet into the sleeves of uz dress coat by mistake, and howling in a voice to wake the dead and half the ward-room officers: "Call the officer of the deck! Pilot-house there," he says, through the mouth-piece, leaning over uz bunk;—"send aft the officer of the deck!" And O'Shay, down below, thinking ut was me, bellers back: "I'll send ye aft the twist of me thumb in yer eye," he says; "come down and lemme out or I'll come up and make a horse-meat sausage of ye!" And about that time I began to hear 'em in extraordinary expeditions on deck, and the orderly hollerin' to split unself, and the master-at-arms running steeple-chases, and I says to meself ut 's time to spill.

And from the hatchway I noticed there was no officer on the bridge, so I reconnoitered the man at the wheel — the one I come up to be standing by to relieve. "The matter?" says he, shifting uz quid and staring straight on in her course —'t was a bright moonlight night, ten miles off Sandy Hook. "There 's the divil to pay and no pitch hot," he says. "Just listen to the old man talking in uz drink through the voice-pipe!" And I took the mouth-piece and heard a voice saying: "I warn ye; if me soul leaves me body I'll come up at ye through the pipe, I will! I'll stick yer heart that full of holes as a strawberry!" he says. " Me naked spirit 'll sit on yer ear," he says, " like a barnacle on a clam — talking to ye till the end of time!" he says, "and longer, begad!"

And me heart moved two inches to one side, for I know'd 't was O'Shay that was bringing the whole ship's company to uts feet with the belief that old Tarrant had gone daft with uz drink. I could hear manding and countermanding from stem to stern of her. With that I grabbed a gallon of valve oil from the floor of the pilot-house and dumped ut quick down the pipe and polished off the mouth-piece with me sleeve. And I tumbled below, for I had but five minutes to git O'Shay and save uz neck from court-martial; and I knew the oil would only stop um till he could spit ut out and draw uz breath. For luck there was no one by when I unfastened um. " Hello, Clarence," says I. " What are ye here for?" " For me health, ye baboon!" says he, spitting oil from uz teeth. And at first he showed fight; but I hauled um out by the collar of uz neck and sat um down hard once or twice on the tank-tops to show um uz legs was too stiff for ut, and I whispered to um of the officers' running around crazy to find um, with their threats of keel-hauling um. And I carried um up the ladder on me back and planted um on deck with care.

Along come a young surgeon looking for what he could find, and says he: " What ails this man?" " Nothing, sir," says I; " he 's fallen down two hatchways and disturbed uz innards, as appears from uz mouth, sir," which was still bubbling oil. And the surgeon says: " Dump um into the sick-bay." Which I did, giving um a pointer to keep mum with uz voice about smuggling uz jug, and advising um to git all the sleep he could; "for I hear," I says, "ye 're to be hanged at the signal-arm at sunrise."

And when I come for me trick at the wheel, on the bridge I see the pilot-house full of ward-room officers, and they had the quartermaster's mate and the man whose relief I was and the wooden-head Scandinavian orderly, questioning all three of um about what they had said; but the Captain they had soothed back to bed. And they could figure no relationship with the statements of them three and what the Captain had said. I heard 'em send for the regulations and I knowed they was considering the steps to be taken when a captain loses uz command by virtue of uz vice of intemperance, for they thought he had drillium trimmins. And from what I heard I see 't was the intention to watch um in the morning and take action according to uz condition; and so they dispersed. And when me trick was done at four o'clock in the morning I lost no time in dropping below to make a clumsy job of repairing the voice-pipe, at the risk of imminent discovery.

'T was four bells of the morning before I had finished ut. I says to meself, I 'll go and be shining brass knobs in the cabin, to take the Squab's place and hear what is said. And the first thing old Tarrant remarks when he opens the door was: " Go tell the officer of the deck to send aft all those men I placed under arrest last night at midnight." Which I did, and the officer hummed and hawed and says: " How does the Captain look this morning?" " How does he look?" says I; " he looks like he had bad sleep last night, sir," I says, "and maybe misleading dreams, with no irreverence to um, sir."

And the officer says: "Hum; go tell um he was mistaken. He placed no man under arrest last night." And when I told old Tarrant that, he did n't fly off uz handle, but looked a bit dazed to umself. "'T was the night before," he says to umself; "yes, never mind, 't was the night before." And he come with false leisure forrard, and see the quartermaster's mate standing on one leg agin the tompion of old ten-inch smoking of uz pipe to beat the stack of a soft-burning Britisher.

"Was ut las night," says the Captain, "I had you aft at midnight?" he says, a bit dubious. "*Me*, sir?" says the mate with uz eyebrows flying up under uz hat; "no, sir, 't was n't me, sir; nor any night, sir." And old Tarrant walked aft again. And 't was the last word any one hear of ut, or of anything that had occurred that night. But during that cruise the color of old Tarrant's beak changed from a flaming turkey red to a decent claret and water; and 't was plain he thought he had the drillium dreams.

Well I went forward and shook O'Shay to wake um. "Beware me naked spirit!" he mutters, half obvious of umself. "Wake up, Clarence," says I, bringing um to umself. "Are ye better this morning, me boy? 'T is twenty-four hours ye laid in a stupor calling out names to beat the divil. Ye 've had a bad case of drillium trimmins, me lad. 'T is a special dispensation ye 're living this day!"

"Is that all of ut?" says Clarence, rolling of uz eyes with relief. "Thank Heaven!" he says. "I dreamed I was being shipped in a tin can to the King of the Man-Eating Isles!"

THE PARLOUS WHOLENESS OF EPHRAIM

15

THE PARLOUS WHOLENESS OF EPHRAIM

OME of the people forgot the admonition about avoiding the main road, and they went by the Junkins place, and were seen by Zendy as she sat at the window sewing pieces of apples on a string. Cory Judd, who scorned riding, walked past without a look — which was perhaps because of his shame at his pride in his new clothes.

"Now, what's Cory Judd all handsomed up for?" said Zendy. "Do you s'pose he'll tramp clear to Boston, same's he threatens?"

Ephraim sat in the wooden rocker with the "Book of Seven Hundred Ailments," which was opened at Ailment No. 440.

"I dunno," replied Ephraim. "You holler down and ask him 'bout that 'Man-and-Beast Salve.' I've got 440 sprouting out 'twixt my shoulder-blades, sure 's you live; and if it strikes in, it 'll lead to 441, and that 'll be my end. I'm going to have another one them spells; for I believe I must of et something."

"I sh' like to come and ketch myself a-hollering to Cory Judd!" said Zendy, casting a glance at the "Book of Ailments." "You 've got forty 'leven salves. I s'pose the next book will be 'The Complete Barn-

yard Physician.' Then you 'll be a-howling 'round
with the pip, and the distemper, and conniption fits.
If I was you I 'd tumble int' the cellar and git a new
set of griefs — you ain't quite miserable enough these
days. Now I *do* wonder what Cory Judd 's a-kiting
so for. I sh' think 't was Fourth July, the way he 's
slicked up ! "

" Mebbe *I* sha'n't ever be slicking up any more," replied Ephraim. " I 'm a pretty faded man, Zendy,
and you don't two thirds realize it. Don't suspect
you will till I 'm took. Here 's 201 I 've had for years,
and 213, and 697, and I felt a touch of 149 this morning, just as plain as your face : 'aching back, dull eye,
shooting pains, pale tongue —'!"

" ' Can't lie awake by night; no appetite after
meals,' " interpolated Zendy. " Overwork 's what 's
done it. Yesterday you cleaned a lamp-chimney; and
day before you wound the old clock. If I was you I
should n't set and watch me sewing apples; might
tucker you out. Now, if there ain't the Spinneys, in
their new wagon, so washed and dressed they dasn't
sneeze ! Do you s'pose it 's Sabbath, and we 've mis-
laid a whole day from this week? What *do* you
s'pose — ? "

" Why can't ye yell to Elziry Spinney to tell her
boy to pull some that yeller-dock root out back their
house?" replied Ephraim. " I kinder hanker after it,
and it drives off 622. I sh' think you could; might
be my dying wish, for all you know. I can feel my
liver palpitating 'bout twice too fast. Zendy, I 'm
persuaded I must of drunk some rain-water that
wa'n't biled. I bet I 'm heaping full of them invis-

ible phenomenous on page 1286—them you can't see without a burning-glass. I 've got a million of 'em plotting and planning inside of me. I tell ye I can see the handwriting on the wall!"

"Well, I vow!" said Zendy. "If you ain't growing peskier and worse every day. You 're juss well 's I be —and you have been these two years. I sh' think you 'd been blowed up in a railroad accident! All you think about is you. Now I sh' juss like to know what the Spinneys—"

"Yuss, I *be* a-getting worse," replied Ephraim. "See how fat I am? It 's the dropsy,—578,—just as noticeable as your nose. But I had n't spoke, because I don't git no sympathy. There ain't a bone in my body but what 's warped with neuraligy; but all you think about is the neighbors."

"Well," said Zendy, with a sigh, "swaller your forty-'leven medicines! You pour 'em all into one now, don't ye? Why don't you take some shingle-nails and cider, 'gainst the general debility breaking out on ye? Land sakes, if there ain't the Stapleses— and them all perked up, too! Ephrum, somebody 's having a time; and you and me ain't invited!"

"Pshaw!" said Ephraim, "Elziry was in yesterday; and she tells everything; and what she don't know 'bout what 's going on ain't so. I wish you had git-up-and-git enough to screech to Anne Staples and git the whereabouts of that doctor feller that proscribes by mail."

"I know what they 're doing," said Zendy, suddenly. "Sed Staples told me some one told her she overheard 'Mandy Dame say 'Lishy Lemly's daughter

15*

give out she wa'n't going to have you to her wedding. Said you always mourned so much 'bout your ailments that it set the whole company 's solemn 's conference. Said she 'd show folks a wedding without one your speeches. Now that 's just it; they 're having that wedding; and I bet the rest of 'em was 'shamed, and went 'round by the lane."

Ephraim had put down the " Book of Ailments."

" But you don't s'pose so?" he said, rising to peer after the wagon with the Staples family sitting starchly in it. "Now folks would n't do that! I don't kinder believe folks would give a wedding nor any kind of time without me: you see I always make a speech, you know. Besides, I give Jerushy Jane Lemly a muskrat skin once; and one time you worked her a fascinator."

"Yuss; but she always did the most at our huskings," said Zendy.

"Yuss; but she always et the most punkin-pie, too; so that 's even," reasoned Ephraim. "You lemme git the paper; mebbe they 's a circus."

"Circus, pshaw!" said Zendy. "You lemme git the telescope!"

Zendy disappeared up-stairs, while Ephraim vainly searched the weekly edition. Zendy was gone for what seemed a long time, and Ephraim called to her, having long professed that climbing to the second story was too much for him. He thought that the loud puffing with which he at length made the ascent was sufficient notification to Zendy of his unusual performance, and that she would express her surprise at his approach; but Zendy made no sign. The trap-door to the roof was open, and the marks of Zendy's shoes were on the dusty ladder.

"Zendy!" called Ephraim. "What do you see? Is it the wedding? Zendy! Zendy, you ain't fallen off the roof, have ye? Now I wonder if that old fool has slid off and broke her neck?" wailed Ephraim in distress. "Zendy!"

"Um!" said Zendy, finally, from above. She was outside, sitting on the ridge-pole, holding the telescope pointed through the trees toward the barn of the Lemly place, a mile in the distance. But she would not tell what she saw.

"You 're too sick a man," she said, grimly. "If I was to tell, you 'd git a spell of 1177."

"Well, I know," said Ephraim. "Jerushy Jane is having that wedding, and I ain't invited. They think I 'm petered out and could n't speechify to set 'em gaping, same 's I used to. Guess I could outwrastle with old Lemly right now. Zendy, you got to walk past the Lemly place,— juss same 's you did n't know we was slighted,— and give 'em lief to put the thing down in black and white. They sha'n't say 't was forgitfulness, b' George! You go right 'long; do you hear?"

"Sha'n't do no such thing," said Zendy. "I shall leave 'em be. I can see 'em one by one putting their teams int' the barn, juss same 's they was 'shamed. Every one of 'em dressed up stiff 's a ramrod. There 's Elziry Spinney; did you ever see any one look so put-together?"

Zendy refused to go and walk by the Lemly place. Ephraim argued that he could n't do it; because such

an exertion would deliver him over to a number of
numbers that always lurked in his constitution, as
she ought to know. Zendy said that he could take
the old pig and ride; which roused Ephraim's feelings to an uncommon pitch. He rapped his stick on
the floor and went down the stairs more quickly than
he had come up, with unpleasant mutterings. Never-
theless Zendy, sitting on the ridge-pole, was not prepared to see him issue from the house and start with
decided steps down the short stretch that led to the
main road. And when, without stopping, he turned
and set off toward the Lemly place, Zendy put the
astonished telescope on him. Ephraim had departed
without taking his several medicines; he had not in
two years walked so far; if he had gone away it had
been after much urging, so that people who asked
him to be present at their weddings thought themselves under an obligation to him, and he had always
driven in a degree of state. It had been rare to find
him farther than the hen-house. Zendy was troubled.

"I don't kinder like it," she said to herself. "I do
s'pose he is kinder poorly, though not 's much so 's he
thinks. It 's unusual; and unusual breeds unusual;
and I 'm scared lest something 'll happen."

What happened first was that Jerusha Jane Lemly,
while her best friends were worrying over her skirts,
looked up the road from her chamber window and
made an exclamation. The people she had seen driving into the barn completed the invited company,
which had been made select by a number of omis-
sions of Jerusha's choosing; but now the tone of the
gathering was threatened by one she did not like.

" Heaps o' wonders!" said Jerusha. "If there ain't
old Ephrum Junkins — pegging 'long the road 's
though he 'd been made whole by faith! Ma! Ma!
There 's old Ephrum Junkins! Now what you going
to do? I sha'n't have him! I sha'n't, if I set up
here till kingdom come!"

The echoing of this statement through the house
brought consternation, as every one knew what Jerusha Jane would n't do when she said she would n't.
Father Elisha at first mildly suggested that they
might as well let Ephraim in, now that he had come
so far. But Mother Lemly put her thumb on him.
She issued warning to the people who were yet outdoors, and they vanished quickly at her command.
The wedding guests inside suddenly found themselves
whispering in the dark, with all the shades drawn,
and information concerning the progress of Ephraim
Junkins in great demand. Some of those outside,
who had failed to get into the barn before it was
locked, ran hither and thither, and finally put themselves away as best they could; and everybody was
saying to himself: "Well I *do* declare!"— at such a
situation. The most unconcerned person near by was
Ephraim. When after a few minutes he reached the
place, he apparently bade fair to pass on without having vouchsafed a glance; but when opposite the front
door he paid it the compliment of a casual notice.
At the same time seemed to arise a feeling that he
ought to stop for a moment and pay his respects to
old Elisha Lemly; though the perfunctoriness of it
was plainly portrayed on Ephraim's face for all who
cared to see. Jerusha Jane, peeping through a pin-

hole she had made in her chamber shade, saw Ephraim knocking at the kitchen door, just as had been his wont in the days before his ailments.

There was no answer to his knocks. Ephraim tried the barn; but all the doors were locked. Then he went around to the front door, to which a freshly-trodden trail led through the long grass in the yard. Pinned to the panel was an envelop, bearing the scrawl:

"*Lemly's folks all went away yesterday.*"

"Now, ain't that strange!" soliloquized Ephraim, in a penetrating voice. "Old 'Lishy must have pulled up stakes and moved his family to the next county."

The door of the long wagon shed had been so hastily fastened that Ephraim opened it with little difficulty, and the effort gave him a chance to prove that his strength had not so wholly departed as people might think. The sound caused considerable rustling in a pile of salt hay inside. In fact, old Silas Ludlow, who was much beholden to Ephraim Junkins for past services in the way of speechmaking,— Silas being blessed with seven daughters,— had, in endeavoring to hide his head, exposed one half of his person.

"Now, who'd a-thought!" said Ephraim, surveying this considerable half. "If there ain't old Silas's pantyloons — all stuffed with salt hay so 's to keep! I 've known 'em for years by that patch, which don't appear except when he steps into his wagon down to the meeting-house. Gone and left his boots sticking into 'em — almost 's natural 's life; looks as though he was kinder anxious 'bout something when he left 'em there — kinder absent-minded and hurried-like.

Now, what sights you do see when you 're all alone and no one to prove it!"

It was getting unduly warm inside the Lemly house, with only the scullery window open. Ezra Dame, who was shortly to be joined in holy matrimony to Jerusha Jane, if only the Lord would make a suitable disposition of Ephraim Junkins, was so embarrassed in his corner that he was smiling painfully; and it was especially hard on the two Lemly poor relations, who toiled in the kitchen, cooking the wedding dinner and growing redder in the face and more hateful of Jerusha every minute. Ephraim had been investigating with leisurely thoroughness; and now he made his way to the front door, and solemnly settled himself on the big stone step. In the parlor the impression gained that he had gone. But now he was plainly heard to say:

"Guess I 'll set and brood awhile."

For some time Ephraim kept eating some choice apples he had discovered near the scullery window.

"Now I will say this is a pretty tearful subject," he began, at length, in a voice as if he was talking to a large assemblage, but all the while looking at the envelop in his hand. "Here 's the whole Lemly fam'ly suddenly took right off the earth—clean sweep. Here 's me a-setting on the door-step, and here 's the old Lemly house shut 's tight 's a drum, and nary soul inside—nary one. Now, ain't that a pity! Here 's the barn-doors closed, and old Lemly forgot and went off and left 'em all padlocked on the inside. I don't see how he ever got out himself, nor how he 's to git in. But I see through a crack they was as many 's

fifteen of his neighbors' hosses crawled in there somehow or other, and it 's a wonder some of their owners
ain't here looking for 'em.   Strange that old Lemly
should go 'way and leave these fancy Baldwins 'round.
Dunno 's they 's anything I like so 's one of his late-
ripe'ing Baldwins, when they 're hard and green,
same 's these; and this was off year for apples, too;
and Simon Staples told me only yesterday how 'Lishy
was saving the only few he had, for some pet purpose,
and here he 's gone away and left 'em!   I sh'll have
to take the rest of 'em home.

"'T is mighty sad to think of the whole Lemly tribe
being wiped off the map of this township in one sun-
down," continued Ephraim, turning to face the darkened windows, "especially that old dried-up Jerushy
Jane, her that we was all afraid would git spliced to
that young nincompoop Ezry Dame.   I 'm glad she 's
quit without so, for that 's a sight of trouble saved.
I 'm glad because, that while 't is generally thought
that while Jerushy Jane — even her — deserves a mite
better than such as him, also Ezry Dame he deserves
a quick sight better than Jerushy Jane.   For the
Lord knows no one would think of marrying her if
't wa'n't for what her father has.   *I* was scared least
they would hitch up, and I be requested to make one
them felicitating speeches, one such as no wedding
has been complete without or thought of in these here-
abouts for the last twenty-five years.   For I should
of had to git out of it the easiest I could, without
hurting some one's feelings, not being cantankerous-
like nor *mean-sneaking* out from a thing, as folks has
been known to.   But I 'd seen Jerushy Jane die an

old maid, which by nature she was meant to do, 'fore
I 'd git up and prognosticate lies 'bout her future
happiness, here or hereafter; for there ain't a person
in this county that can see how any one is to be con-
gratulated for marrying Jerushy Jane, nor any one
for marrying Ezry Dame."

In the parlor old Peter Hammond, while waiting
for the ceremony to begin, had fallen asleep. Ezra
Dame was so red that he thought his cheeks visible in
the dark—a thought which made them redder.

" So they 's a sorter sweet sorrer in that," pursued
Ephraim, "though it does seem pretty tearful to have
the whole Lemly fam'ly took out from under your
feet like a stroke of lightning. They must of left in
a hurry, for they did n't stop to take in the mats from
the doors, but left out their best one, which I ain't
seen before since I give it to Mother Lemly when she
and 'Lishy had their silver wedding. Pretty expen-
sive mat that was—as any one could see by comparing
it to the one 'Lishy bought to give the minister when
he was married. Mother Lemly, I hear, used this one
for a tidy at first. She 'd never gone and left it lying
loose like this unless 't was something happened—
mebbe she heard of some one that was willing to
marry Jerushy; and as for 'Lishy, Lord knows he
would n't leave a hoss-hair 'round if he thought an
angel might take it for a harp-string. And they left
the scullery window open. Awful absent-minded,"
said Ephraim, rising. " Thieves might break in and
steal Jerushy's curls."

The remainder of the late-ripening Baldwins had
disappeared from the scullery window; but Ephraim

did not seem to notice it. He took away the stick
that held the sash up, and closed the window, leaving the two poor relations to stifle in the kitchen.
In the parlor the minister was staring devoutly at
the points of sunlight that came through the win-
dow-shade to which Ephraim was now addressing
his meditations. Every one was unaware of Ephraim, and determined that every one else should
perceive it.

"Beats all," continued Ephraim loudly, as he settled himself once more on the stone step, "how things
without spiritual life shows how they miss Jerushy!
'T is juss so everything that belongs to the fam'ly
could speak. 'Here,' says this envelop, which I see
is postmarked this morning, and could n't of got
here before this noon —'here,' says it, 'Ephrum Junkins must know 'bout this.' So it shakes the letter
from its inwards, and runs and gits a pencil and
scratches on its back: 'Lemly's folks all went away
yesterday,' in a first-rate forgery of Mother Lemly's
handwriting; and then climbs up and pins itself to
the door. Juss the same with the things out back.
'Here,' says they, 'Jerushy Jane 's gone off looking
for some wooden-head to marry her; but we 'll git
ourselves ready 'gainst her coming back unsuccessful,
juss same 's them two poor relations of hers, that
does all the work and gits nothing for it but leav-
ings and hard words, same 's they was here to slop
'round and get dinner.' So them late-ripe'ing Baldwins says to themselves: 'Here, we 'd better git in
out the sun, or we 'll git mellered 'fore our time.'
So they up and roll int' the house, same 's they had

legs. Then the sink-pump begins to draw water,— I
can hear it a-snorting now,— sounds juss 's though
old Peter Hammond was setting in the corner of the
parlor winder and had fell asleep waiting for something to happen. Then out back the shed some that
wood that 'Lishy cut from widder Cole's half-acre,
because she could n't pay the interest on the mort-
gage, and he knew the church would git her through
the winter somehow — some that wood takes the ax
and chops itself to kindlings, and gits a match and
crawls int' the stove, and touches itself off and roars
like a turkey-red lion, as you can see by the smoke
a-spilling out the chimney. 'Jerushy Jane 'll be
home 'for' long,' says everything. And the old
black pot gits down off the hook, and waddles up to
the sink and gits itself full of water, and climbs up
on the stove, and sets down to git a-bubbling. And
then the onions,— I can smell 'em 's loud 's they
was under my chin,— well, they turn to and peel off
their coats, and run and jump int' the pot, and squat
down to bile!

"Still," said Ephraim, very loudly, "I dunno why
I sh'd be brooding here. The Lemlys ain't much to
me. I always treated 'em considerate like. When
Mother Lemly come to me and said what a close-
fisted old barn-rat 'Lishy was, I never told 'Lishy.
When 'Lishy come to me and asked if 't was wicked
to wish that Mother Lemly was enjoying a stay in
Heaven, I never told her. I give 'em both my honest
sympathy; but they ain't anything to me — more than
folks that live in the same town that I do. First
thing I know my folks from Boston will be arriving;

and I dunno 's I 'd pick out juss these steps to let 'em
see me setting on; for my Boston folks are pretty
tony and stylish, and rather particular 'bout who
they see me with. I 'll make that stretch home in
'bout nine minutes."

Ephraim straightened himself and walked briskly
from the yard, and still more briskly until he had
gone from sight around a bend in the road. The exercise, far from fatiguing him, was exhilarating; and
he kept on at the same gait, chuckling as he went.
The stick with which he had plodded up the stairs to
find Zendy lay forgotten in the Lemly yard. Ephraim grew more charmed with himself at every step.

Zendy was standing alone. The figure that seemed
to be Ephraim was coming too fast for him, and when
Ephraim was within call he did not seem himself; for
the customary melancholy of his face was supplanted
by a gleam of satisfaction. Zendy was troubled.

"What 's the matter?" she said. "Where you
been? Where 's your stick? Ain't you tuckered?"

"Well, sir," said Ephraim, radiantly, steaming past
her and taking the rise in front of the house at a pace
which left her in the rear. "Well, sir, I juss give it
to 'em! Guess they won't forgit it! Is anybody fol-
lering me — ? 'Cause I ain't looked 'round;— walked
off juss same 's I forgotten 'em at their own gate.
You oughter heard me a-brooding aloud — offhand!
'Onions took their coats off,' says I, 'and jumped in
and squat down to bile!' Plain 's your face! And
Silas's Sunday pantyloons — hee, hee! Well, sir,
you 'll wish you 'd come!"

"There, Ephraim, there," said Zendy, soothingly.

"You ain't quite well, I 'm sure. You 're all tuck-ered, ain't ye? There, I should n't let myself git so excited. How 's your aches?"

"Tuckered?" said Ephraim. "Who 's tuckered? I 'll teach 'em I ain't no setting rooster, b' George! Think I 've lost my gift, do they? As for aches and pains, I ain't a single one — if I was to try. Dunno 's I ever shall have again. I 've shook my ills and give up pills — and don't pay no more doctor's bills, — eh, Zendy?"

"Ephrum Junkins," said Zendy, solemnly, "you 've got to git right to bed! You 're a sick man; and you don't realize it one mite. I ain't seen you exert so these ten years! Don't you lemme hear 'nother word. You need every parcel of strength you got. Oh, Eph-rum, why did n't you stay to home?"

"Go-to-bed pshaw!" said Ephraim. "I tell ye I 'm 's pert 's a sparrer. Could n't find no ache nor pain if I was to hunt."

"That 's juss what 's the matter," said Zendy. "You 've come to the fair hill-top overlooking the valley of shadder of death, Ephrum, and here you be a-ready to go coasting down t' the bottom 's fast 's you know how! Don't you see how 't always is? — them that's ailing all of a sudden gitting up and hop-ping round outdoors and looking pert, and everybody saying how smart Ephrum Junkins is looking — and then all of a jump the Lord whisks your head off 's though 't was an ax. Ephrum — I dunno, Ephrum! There," she said, recovering herself; "you go to bed, won't ye?"

"Pshaw!" said Ephraim. "Here I be as skittish

16

as a yeller kitten. You sh'd see me kiting 'long the
road, 's though I was shot from a bow! Well, sir,
they was fifteen hosses that crawled int' that barn,
b' George; and they 'd locked themselves in — eh?
I s'pose I set there 's much 's an hour — brooding
to myself loud enough for the pigeons. I callate
Jerushy Jane 'll live to see me — "

But the enthusiasm had spilled from Ephraim's
voice.

"I *was* going to step off front the house 'bout time
the wedding broke off, and chop that tree I been a-
going to so long," he added, thoughtfully.

Zendy left him sitting still in the rocking-chair,
gazing rather steadily at his thumbs. She ran down
to the road and caught the boy whom she had seen
driving one of Lemly's teams.

"You hurry and find Doctor Payne," she said.
"He's down to the wedding, I guess. You tell him to
come up along 's fast 's he can; for Ephrum Junkins
is took so that I misdoubt he 'll last the evening.
You hurry and I 'll give you a watermelon."

When she came back Ephraim was silent, and she
looked at him sadly and said nothing. He expected
her to urge him again to retire; but she did not.
At length Ephraim said:

"Of course, if you 're any scared, Zendy, I s'pose I
might just as well go. Still, it does seem kinder
foolish; and I should n't tell any the neighbors 'bout
it."

"Hain't you the leetlest kind of an ache?" asked
Zendy.

"No," said Ephraim, with a shade of regret. "I

can't truthfully git up and lie 'bout it. I ain't got
the shadder of one."

"It 's unusual," said Zendy; "and unusual breeds
unusual. You jump in 's quick 's you know how;
and I 'll make a poultice and some licorish tea; and
I 'll stuff your ears with cotton, so the crickets and
roosters and things sha'n't keep you awake. And
there, I 'd drink some hot water if I was you. Dunno 's I should be scared, Ephraim; mebbe it 'll pass
off in the night."

Ephraim lay in the depths of the feather-bed, with
the blinds closed, while Zendy stirred about the ad-
joining kitchen. A streak of sunlight came through
and found the wall beside him; all the world seemed
wide awake and well; but Ephraim's lightsome spirits
had departed. Presently he called:

"'T is kinder unusual, ain't it?"

"Well, mebbe," said Zendy. "Still —"

"Still what?" said Ephraim, with the cotton in his
ears. "Say, I guess you 'd better git out some that
Mrs. Slopley's Sure Cure — 't won't do no harm;
though I dunno 's they 's any cause for you to git
worried, feeling so smart 's I do —?"

"Oh no," said Zendy; "worrying will only make
you worse."

Ephraim lay staring at the ceiling, unpleasantly
aware of his own fiber. He listened to the throbbing
of his arteries and asked himself if there was not
something unusual in it — unusual bred unusual.
People's hearts sometimes unexpectedly stopped, and
then people gave three gasps and all was over.

"S'pose you set some that Greenson's Painkiller

handy," he called. "And if you sh'd see Doctor
Payne you might yell to him. I felt 's coltish 's a
calf when I laid down here; but I dunno."

The ticking of the clock seemed to keep time with
his breathing — at least it had at first; but now
surely the clock was getting ahead. His lungs might
be gradually slowing down, and perhaps they would
lag until by and by they would stop short — collapsed like an empty bellows.

"I dunno but you 'd better send for him, Zendy —
so 's to keep you from worrying," he managed to say
without falling behind the clock.

"There, I should n't snort so," said Zendy. "He 's
a-coming."

"What, you sent for him?" exclaimed Ephraim.
"I wonder if you 've had one your presentiments? I
should n't have such nonsense. Here I be, looking 's
bright 's a new dollar — ain't I? What 's the use
you trying to scare me so? There, ain't that clock
gitting ready to stop? I ain't superstitious; but you
kinder make me nervous running 'round the way
you do."

Zendy comforted him with the licorice tea for his
inner man, and with something she put between his
shoulders — a poultice the mustardy nature of which
she concealed from Ephraim on account of his objec-
tion to being burned. The licorice tea began searching for the late-ripening Baldwins.

Lemly's boy had met the people as they were leaving after the wedding, and he mingled among them,
eager with the importance of his news; so that before dusk every one had heard of Ephraim's going to

bed. Those who had known Ephraim and Zendy since early years came in to see if they could be of assistance; and they made a considerable gathering of people in their Sunday clothes.

"I ain't going to be caught napping," exclaimed Zendy. "Here he ails and wails every minute for two years, and here he gits up suddenly and tramps off somewhere, and says he ain't got an ache nor a pain, and wants to chop down trees! I juss drove him to bed."

Ephraim removed the cotton from one ear. The arrival of the visitors had for awhile turned his thoughts away from himself.

"Real nice of you to put your good clothes on juss to come see us," he heard Zendy say. They all sat in the kitchen, with the lamp casting a dimness over their faces; and they settled themselves as if they had come to see the affair to its end. Conversation languished; for everybody was thinking about the wedding, and no one dared to speak of it. Old Peter Hammond, who was deaf, was last; and Ephraim heard him say:

"What — nary an ache nor pain?"

"Nary a fly-bite," called Ephraim. "I dunno 'f the Lord 's crowding a place for me on the other shore; but seems to me 't would of been juss as well if I 'd first stepped out front and chopped that old apple-tree. Been going to these ten years; ever since the time Leviticus Brooks drove the pitchfork into his leg, and Alice Dame 's calf got hurt, too, and Joel Pitkin was 'lected."

"He 's beginning to reach back," whispered Amanda

16ᵃ

Dame to Sarah Tower. "When they begin to reach back years and years, then I know they 're going out."

This remark was repeated to the others; and for a while Ephraim heard nothing but an ominous murmur.

"Good deal of sickness and ailments 'round," came the voice of Mother Margery Hook, at length breaking the funereal silence. "They do say May Tenny Warren won't last out the night — and she so young, too, — you would n't expect. And then old Jeddy Marvin — that was born on same day 's Ephraim — he 's done a fearful night and ain't no better. I declare I ain't got nothing fit to wear to a funeral."

"You 'll have to go just to weddings till you git something new," said Zendy, surveying Mother Margery's lavender trimmings. This remark caused another silence.

"Zendy!" called Ephraim. "You steep me some that catnip, will ye?"

"What she said reminds me of old Josiah Codman," came the voice of Hannah Swan. "Old Josiah, 'f you remember, rose up from a stroke and hoed a whole patch of beets. Come evening he was flat on his back; and stone cold before morning."

Ephraim's mind went back to the clock, which now seemed to tarry behind his breathing. Perhaps his lungs would go faster and faster, until they burst with panting, and he lay stone dead.

"There was Jim Sweet's wife, too," he heard Angy Brooks say. "She left the chronic sinking-fits and went to a dance. Said she 'd like to see the one that could outbob and fling with her! And she up and died in the middle of a jig. Most of the orthodox folks took it for a judgment."

"Then Eunice Dexter, 'f you remember," said Hannah Swan —" she that married the Spooner twins, one after the other. She got up and went to a husking, and died from eating Mother Hammond's pandowdy. I don't s'pose Ephrum 's et anything, has he ?"

"No," said Zendy; "he ain't et anything; he 's too scared to eat what fights him." But Ephraim thought of the late-ripening Baldwins; and for some indefinable reason he wished he had not touched them.

"Zendy !" he called. "That boy ain't found Doctor Payne! Why 's he so slow ?"

"Doctor Payne?" said Mother Margery Hook. "Gone to Boston — for a week."

"Thunder !" said Ephraim, breaking out in a cold sweat. "Zendy, what you going to do ?"

"And Doctor Wallace is away to Bucksport," whispered Peter Hammond, loudly. "Still, I don't think a doctor would mend any, Zendy. I quit doctoring these ten years. Speaking of like cases," Ephraim heard Peter say, "come to think of it, there was Ephrum's own father. 'T was juss 'bout same 's this. Dunno 's any of you remember; but old Ephrum had been lain up with something he called typhoid-gout,— he doctored himself mostly,— and one day he rose off his lounge, where he 'd been most the time for several years, carving little clipper ships inside of ginger-pop bottles, rose off and took stick and stumped clear down to Cedar Creek; and

made old Enoch Blood,—that was keeping a black-
smith shop 'bout where the meeting-house now is,—
made him pone up seven dollars Enoch had owed him
since he 'd married Thankful Spinney — with seven
per cent. interest — and had them four boys. And
old Ephrum come a-thumping home all smiling 's
could be, and said he callated to git out to work to
his trade — which, if you rec'lect, was shipwright.
Well, come lamplight,—'bout this time 's I remember,
— he was suddenly took with a cramp somewhere in
his inwards; and old Ephrum juss wriggled himself
out of this world — you 'd heard him for miles. He
had three doctors; but Lord, the doctors could n't
do him no good! So Ephrum need n't feel so bad."

"Zendy," called Ephraim, feebly, with beads upon
his brow. "My inwards don't feel right. S'pose I
take some Fam'ly Cure? I think mebbe I have a
pain."

Zendy absented herself for awhile, during which
she conned the symptoms of Ephraim with a practised eye. Then she came out and whispered to the
rest.

"His eyes are kinder staring, and his breath comes
quick, and his hair kinder stands up; but Lord, I ain't
worried no more. He ain't going to sink. No, he
ain't; I know Ephrum."

"I dunno 's I sh'd be too hopeful," Ephraim heard
Mother Margery say; and Peter Hammond whispered
very plainly: "Neither sh'd I — with that pain — so
like his father."

"Zendy!" called Ephraim. "440 's commencing
to burn betwixt my shoulder-blades. I wish some of

you 'd look into the book. Zendy ain't worth a hill of beans with it."

Peter Hammond had the book in his grasp, and no one could get it away from him.

"Here 's 440," said Peter, after a search which had led him to page 440 instead of to the ailment of that number. "Some kinder fits, it says; but pshaw, Ephrum, it don't say they break out 'twixt your shoulder-blades."

"Zendy — ain't you a gump!" cried Ephraim. "Give the book to some one that can spell numbers. Have I got to lay here and die! Oh, my back! Oh, but I 'm a sick man!"

Zendy returned to the chamber. Ephraim lay with his face pushed into the pillow.

"My time 's come," he cried in muffled tones. "I can feel myself stiflin'. I 'm a-goin'; 201 's comin' back; 697 's comin'; 440 's bringin' on 441! I 'm a-goin'; good-by, Zendy, if I sh'd lose my mind!"

Zendy came and closed the door. The visitors stared expectantly.

"I guess you folks had better all go home," she said, "unless you got some wedding or other to go to; for it kinder flusters Ephrum. He 's all right now. He 's got his aches and pains back; and he 's too strapping mad and scared with his ailments to be a-going to die. Good-night, all," she said, as she held the lamp and they filed out into the dark. "I kinder put faith in that mustard and licorish." But it was plain that they all thought Ephraim in a perilous state.

Ephraim was rolling and writhing in the billows of

the feather-bed. Zendy hove a sigh of relief to see him; and she sat down and rested in the wooden rocker.

"There, if you ain't carrying on natural," she said, approvingly. "Just as like yourself as two peas. There, I dunno 's I 'd shout so."

"I was ticketed to leave ye 'fore long!" cried Ephraim. "I kep' tellin' ye so, but I did n't git no sympathy. 440 has struck in! Zendy, why don't you git scared and do somethin'? Here I be on my dyin' bed, and you a-settin' there like a bump on a log! Oh, them apples — my back 's burnin' right off! Oh, Zendy, ain't you got no more feeling than I was a frog?"

The head of Cory Judd appeared at the open window.

"Heard Ephrum was took," said Cory, who sometimes looked like an owl. "How 's he doing?"

"Oh, he 's doing real nice, thank ye," said Zendy. "I guess he only et something."

"Oh, yuss!" said Ephraim, savagely, rising in bed. "I was invited out to a wedding; and I et the door-knob off the door!"

www.ingramcontent.com/pod-product-compliance
Lightning Source LLC
Chambersburg PA
CBHW031345020726
47499CB00005B/1413